I0607105

Chas. Steigerwalt

Catalogue of a $12,000 Collection

Of Choice United States and Foreign Coins, Paper Money, Medals

Chas. Steigerwalt

Catalogue of a $12,000 Collection
Of Choice United States and Foreign Coins, Paper Money, Medals

ISBN/EAN: 9783742832085

Manufactured in Europe, USA, Canada, Australia, Japa

Cover: Foto ©Andreas Hilbeck / pixelio.de

Manufactured and distributed by brebook publishing software
(www.brebook.com)

Chas. Steigerwalt

Catalogue of a $12,000 Collection

CATALOGUE

OF A

$12,000 COLLECTION

OF

CHOICE UNITED STATES AND FOREIGN COINS, PAPER MONEY, MEDALS, ETC.

For Sale by CHAS. STEIGERWALT,

130 East King Street, Lancaster, Pa.

No. 34.   ESTABLISHED 1878.   Oct. and Nov., 1892.

REMARKS.

Please Read. Send orders early to prevent disappointment. Do not order anything you have not a reasonable expectation of buying if found correct, and return anything not desired as soon as possible after receipt of goods. Some of the coins, etc., in this list are out on approval now, but are included, as they may be returned. Coins sent on approval to responsible buyers. Remittances should be made by Money Order, Postal Note, Registered Letter, Check or Draft. Don't send stamps of high values. Address all letters plainly, and make money orders, etc., payable to Chas. Steigerwalt, 130 East King Street, Lancaster, Pa.

Note. This collection is particularly choice, and is the largest ever offered for sale at fixed prices. It contains many gems, and all the rarities in the U. S. silver and copper series, except the 1804 dollar. In addition will be found choice lines of paper money, foreign gold, silver and copper coins, ancient coins, medals, numismatic books, curios, etc. The prices have been made very low.

United States Gold.

1868. Double Eagle. Br. proof. 22.00.
1795. Eagle. Very fine. 17.50.
1796. Eagle. Fine and scarce. 17.50.
1797. Eagle. Extremely fine. 13.00.
1797. Eagle. *Four stars facing.* About uncirculated. Semi-proof surface. Extra rare. 75.00.
1798. Over '97. Eagle. *Four stars facing.* Very fine and rare. 50.00.

1798. Over '97. Eagle. Six stars facing. But little circulated.
       Excessively rare. 85.00.
1799. Eagle. Fine. 11.50.
1800. Eagle. Barely circulated. Mint bloom. 16.00.
1801. Eagle. Barely circulated. Mint bloom. 13.50.
1803. Eagle. Barely circulated. Mint bloom. 13.50.
1804. Eagle. But little circulated. Mint bloom. Profile weak.
       30.00.
1795. Half Eagle. Extremely fine. 12.50.
1796 over '95. Half Eagle. Very fine. 25.00.
1798. Half Eagle. Fine. 7.50.
1800. Half Eagle. Uncirculated. Brilliant mint bloom. 7.50.
1802. Over '01. Half Eagle. About uncirculated, slight proof
       surface. 7.00.
1803. Over '02. Half Eagle. Nearly uncirculated, slight proof
       surface. 7.00.
1804. Half Eagle. Barely circulated. Mint bloom. 7.50.
1805. Half Eagle. Extremely fine. 7.00.
1806. Half Eagle. Blunt 6. Extremely fine. Lustre. 6.50.
1807. Half Eagle. Head to right. Fine. 6.50.
1807. Half Eagle. Head to left. Uncirculated. Mint bloom.
       7.50.
1809. Half Eagle. Barely circulated. Mint bloom. 6.50.
1810. Half Eagle. Uncirculated. Mint bloom. 7.00.
1811. Half Eagle. Uncirculated. 7.00.
1812. Half Eagle. Barely circulated. Mint bloom. 6.50.
1813. Half Eagle. Uncirculated. 7.00.
1814. Half Eagle. Uncirculated. Mint bloom. Sharp. 9.00.
1818. Half Eagle. Uncirculated. Mint bloom. 8.50.
1820. Half Eagle. Uncirculated. Mint bloom. Rare. 20.00.
1823. Half Eagle. Uncirculated. Brilliant mint lustre. 20.00.
1826. Half Eagle. Uncirculated. Very rare. 25.00.
1834. Half Eagle. Old type. Uncirculated. Bold impression.
       Brilliant mint lustre. 15.00.
1863. Three Dollars. Barely circulated. 6.00.
1871. Three Dollars. Barely circulated. 4.00.
1874. Three Dollars. Barely circulated. 4.00.
1877. Three Dollars. Uncirculated. Some proof surface. 5.00.
1878. Three Dollars. Uncirculated. Mint bloom. 4.00.
1881. Three Dollars. Uncirculated. Semi-proof. 4.00.
1882. Three Dollars. Brilliant proof. 5.00.
1883. Three Dollars. Brilliant proof. 5.00.
1884. Three Dollars. Brilliant proof. 5.00.
1885. Three Dollars. Brilliant proof. 5.00.
1886. Three Dollars. Brilliant proof. 5.00.
1887. Three Dollars. Brilliant proof. 5.00.
1888. Three dollars. Brilliant proof. 5.00.
1889. Three Dollars. Brilliant proof. 5.00.

1796. Quarter Eagle. *With stars.* Scarcely touched by circulation, semi-proof. Scarcely perceptible pin scratch across face. Excessively rare. 60.00.
1797. Quarter Eagle. Very fine. 50.00.
1798. Quarter Eagle. Uncirculated. Mint bloom. Proof surface. 20.00.
1802. Quarter Eagle. About a brilliant proof. 12.50.
1804. Quarter Eagle. Barely circulated. 8.50.
1805. Quarter Eagle. Barely circulated. Brilliant mint bloom. 8.50.
1806 over '04. Quarter Eagle. Centre not well struck up (all that way), otherwise sharp impression. Brilliant mint lustre, semi-proof surface. Extremely rare. 50.00.
1806 over '05. Quarter Eagle. Extra fine. Excessively rare. 50.00.
1807. Quarter Eagle. Very fine. 7.50.
1808. Quarter Eagle. Fine. 6.00.
1824. Quarter Eagle. Barely if any circulated. 17.50.
1825. Quarter Eagle. Uncirculated. Semi-proof. 20.00.
1827. Quarter Eagle. Uncirculated. Brilliant mint lustre. 20.00.
1829. Quarter Eagle. Uncirculated, some proof surface. 12.50.
1830. Quarter Eagle. Uncirculated. Semi-proof surface. 6.00.
1831. Quarter Eagle. *Brilliant proof.* 12.00.
1832. Quarter Eagle. Uncirculated. Brilliant mint bloom. 7.50.
1833. Quarter Eagle. Uncirculated. Brilliant mint bloom. 12.50.
1834. Quarter Eagle. *Brilliant proof.* 5.00.
1835. Quarter Eagle. Semi-proof. Handsome. 4.00.
1836. Quarter Eagle. Uncirculated. Brilliant mint bloom. 3.50.
1838. Quarter Eagle. Uncirculated. Brilliant mint bloom. 3.50.
1839. Quarter Eagle. C. Mint. But little circulated. 3.50.
1840, 1841, 1846, 1849. Quarter Eagles. D. M. Very fine. Each 3.00.
1843. Quarter Eagle. D. Mint. But little circulated. 3.50.
1844. Quarter Eagle. D. M. Uncirculated. Mint bloom. 4.00.
1861. Quarter Eagle. Uncirculated. 3.00.
1863. Quarter Eagle. S. M. Very fine. 3.00.
1875. Quarter Eagle. Brilliant proof. 5.00.
1876. Quarter Eagle. Brilliant proof. 5.00.
1880. Quarter Eagle Brilliant proof. 3.50.
1881. Quarter Eagle. Brilliant proof. 3.50.
1882. Quarter Eagle. Brilliant proof. 3.50.
1883. Quarter Eagle. Brilliant proof. 3.50.
1884. Quarter Eagle. Brilliant proof. 3.50.
1885. Quarter Eagle. Brilliant proof. 3.50.
1886. Quarter Eagle. Brilliant proof. 3.50.
1887. Quarter Eagle. Brilliant proof. 3.50.
1888. Quarter Eagle. Brilliant proof. 3.50.
1889. Quarter Eagle. Brilliant proof. 3.50.
1841. Dollar. Uncirculated. Sharp little beauty. 2.50.

1859. Dollar. Uncirculated. 2.50.
1850. Dollar. Uncirculated. Sharp little beauty. 2.50.
1852. Dollar. Uncirculated. Sharp little beauty. 2.50.
1853. Dollar. Uncirculated. Sharp little beauty. 2.50.
1854. Dollar. Small. Uncirculated. Sharp little beauty. 2.50.
1854. Dollar. Large. Uncirculated. 2.00.
1855. Dollar. Brilliant proof. 12.50.
1855. Dollar. Uncirculated. 2.00.
1856. Dollar. Brilliant proof. 12.50.
1856. Dollar. Small date. Straight 5. Barely circulated. 2.50.
1856. Dollar. Large date. Slanting 5. Uncirculated. 2.00.
1857. Dollar. Uncirculated. 2.00.
1859. Dollar. Uncirculated. 2.00.
1860. Dollar. Brilliant proof. 5.00.
1860. Dollar. Uncirculated. 2.50.
1861. Dollar. Brilliant proof. 5.00.
1861. Dollar. Uncirculated. 2.50.
1862. Dollar. Uncirculated. 2.00.
1864. Dollar. Uncirculated. Brilliant mint bloom. 17.50.
1865. Dollar. Uncirculated. Semi-proof. 10.00.
1866. Dollar. Uncirculated. Semi-proof. 7.50.
1867. Dollar. Uncirculated. Semi-proof. 5.00.
1868. Dollar. Brilliant proof. 5.00.
1869. Dollar. Uncirculated. Brilliant mint bloom. 5.00.
1870. Dollar. Brilliant proof. 5.00.
1871. Dollar. Uncirculated. Brilliant mint bloom. 3.50.
1872. Dollar. Proof. 5.00.
1873. Dollar. Uncirculated. Brilliant. 2.00.
1874. Dollar. Uncirculated. Brilliant. 2.00.
1876. Dollar. Brilliant proof. 7.50.
1877. Dollar. Proof. 4.00.
1878. Dollar. Uncirculated. Brilliant. 2.00.
1879. Dollar. Brilliant proof. 2.50.
1880. Dollar. Semi-proof. 2.00.
1881. Dollar. Brilliant proof. 2.50.
1882. Dollar. Brilliant proof. 2.50.
1883. Dollar. Brilliant proof. 2.50.
1884. Dollar. Brilliant proof. 2.50.
1885. Dollar. Brilliant proof. 2.50.
1886. Dollar. Brilliant proof. 2.50.
1887. Dollar. Brilliant proof. 2.50.
1888. Dollar. Brilliant proof. 2.50.
1889. Dollar. Uncirculated. Brilliant. 2.00.
1849. Dollar. O. Mint. Barely circulated. 2.00.
1849. Dollar. D. Mint. Very fine. 3.00.
1850. Dollar. O. Mint. Very fine. 3.00.
1851. Dollar. O. Mint. Barely circulated. 2.00.
1851. Dollar. C. Mint. Extremely fine. 3.00.

1852. Dollar. O. Mint. Extremely fine. 2.00.
1853. Dollar. O. Mint. Extremely fine. 2.00.
1853. Dollar. C. Mint. Very fine. 3.00.
1855. Dollar. O. Mint. Extremely fine. 2.50.
1855. Dollar. C. Mint. Fine. 2.50.
1856. Dollar. S. Mint. *Small head of 1855.* Extremely fine. 3.50.
1859. Dollar. C. Mint. Very fine. 3.00.
1859. Dollar. D. Mint. Extremely fine. 3.50.
1859. Dollar. S. Mint. Extremely fine. 3.50.
1860. Dollar. S. Mint. Very fine, but pierced. 2.00.
Georgia. "C. Bechtler at Rutherford. 5 Dollars." Rev.,
    "Georgia Gold. 128 G. 22 carats." Semi-proof. 10.00.
Carolina. "A. Bechtler. Rutherford." 5 Dollars. Fine. 7.00.
Carolina. "A. Bechtler." Dollar. About uncirculated. 2.00.

Collection of U. S. Gold Dollars.

U. S. Gold Dollars. Complete collection from 1849 to 1889 (both 1854's). 42 pcs. The collection is in very nice condition, being nearly all in uncirculated or brilliant proof condition. Proofs are 1866, 1867, 1868, 1872, 1873, 1874, 1875, 1877, 1879 to 1888: the 1863, 1864, 1865 and balance of the set, with a few exceptions and these but little worn, are uncirculated. Very neatly mounted on velvet backing in a handsome mottled wood circular frame with plate glass front. 150.00.

United States Proof Sets.

1846. Proof Set. Contains Dollar, Half Dollar, Quarter, Dime, Half Dime, and two Copper Cents (the tall 6 and the "Dutch 6.") and Half Cent (original). The "Dutch 6" cent is sharp and perfect, but not as brilliant as proofs of later years, but the rest of the set is in nice condition. The Dime and Half Dime are beauties, and very rare in this condition. 100.00.
1857. Proof Set. Similar to last. 50.00.
1858. Proof Set. 7 pcs. 65.00.
1859. Proof Set. 7 pcs. 6.00.
1860. Proof Set. 7 pcs. 6.00.
1861. Proof Set. 7 pcs. 6.00.
1862. Proof Set. 7 pcs. 6.00.
1863. Proof Set. 7 pcs. 6.00.
1864. Proof Set. 9 pcs. 10.00.
1865. Proof Set. 9 pcs. 8.00.
1866. Proof Set. 10 pcs. 6.00.
1867. Proof Set. 10 pcs. 6.00.
1868. Proof Set. 10 pcs. 6.00.
1869. Proof Set. 10 pcs. 5.00.
1870. Proof Set. 10 pcs. 5.00.

1871. Proof Set. 10 pcs. 5.00.
1872. Proof Set. 10 pcs. 5.00.
1873. Proof Set. Old Style. 10 pcs. 6.50.
1873. Proof Set. Trade. 7 pcs. 5.00.
1874. Proof Set. 7 pcs. 5.00.
1875. Proof Set. 8 pcs. 5.00.
1876. Proof Set. 8 pcs. 5.00.
1877. Proof Set. 8 pcs. 9.00.
1878. Proof Set. Includes both dollars and the rare 20 cent. 6.00.
1879. Proof Set. Both dollars. 4.00.
1880. Proof Set. Both dollars. 4.00.
1881. Proof Set. Both dollars. 4.50.
1882. Proof Set. Both dollars. 4.50.
1883. Proof Set. Both dollars. 4.50.
1884. Proof Set. 4.00.
1885. Proof Set. 4.00.
1886. Proof Set. 4.00.
1887. Proof Set. 4.00.
1888. Proof Set. 4.00.
1889. Proof Set. 4.00.
1890. Proof Set. 3.50.
1891. Proof Set. 3.50.
1892. Proof Set. 3.50.

United States Dollars.

1794. Very fine. An unusually even impression : stars, head and date well struck, as is also the reverse. 125.00.
1795. Flowing hair. Very handsome specimen with semi-proof surface. Uncirculated. A gem. 35.00.
1795. Flowing hair. A beautiful specimen. Barely touched. Mint lustre. 15.00.
1795. Fillet head. Uncirculated. Proof surface. 75.00.
1795. Fillet head. Shows scarcely a trace of circulation. Sharp and with considerable lustre. 30.00.
1795. Fillet head. Almost equal to last. 20.00.
1796. Large date. Barely circulated. Considerable lustre. 25.00.
1796. Large date. Quite fine. 5.00.
1796. Small date. Very fine. 7.50.
1797. Seven stars facing. Not a strong impression, but showing but little wear, the feathers on eagle's breast barely touched. 15.00.
1797. Seven stars facing. Very fine. 7.50.
1797. Six stars facing. Uncirculated. Brilliant mint lustre. 35.00.
1797. Six stars facing. Very fine. 7.50.
1798. Fifteen stars. *Small eagle.* Fine. 10.00.
1798. Thirteen stars. *Small eagle.* Very fine. 7.50.

798. Large eagle. But little circulated. Some lustre. 3.00.
799. *Five stars facing.* Fine. 5.00.
799. Strictly uncirculated. Brilliant mint bloom. 5.00.
800. Barest touch of circulation. Brilliant mint bloom. 8.50.
801. Barest touch of circulation. Brilliant mint bloom. 20.00.
802. Uncirculated. Brilliant mint bloom. 25.00.
802. Barely touched on most prominent parts. Mint bloom. 10.00.
802 over '01. Scarcely a touch of circulation. Brilliant mint bloom. 15.00.
803. Large 3. Barely circulated. Sharp, with semi-proof surface. 15.00.
803. Small 3. Very trifling circulation. Brilliant mint bloom. Scarce variety. 10.00.
836. Brilliant proof. Sharp and handsome. 15.00.
836. *Gobrecht in field.* Dull proof. 40.00.
838. *Brilliant proof.* 85.00.
839. *Brilliant proof.* 60.00.
840. *Brilliant proof.* 15.00.
840. Uncirculated. Proof surface. 3.50.
841. Uncirculated. Mint bloom. Semi-proof. 3.00.
842. Uncirculated. Mint bloom. 2.00.
843. Uncirculated. Mint bloom. 2.00.
844. *Brilliant proof.* 20.00.
844. Uncirculated. Mint bloom. 3.50.
845. *Brilliant proof.* A few light haymarks. 15.00.
846. Uncirculated. Mint bloom. 2.50.
846. O. Mint. Barely touched. Mint bloom. Semi-proof surface. 3.50.
847. *Brilliant proof.* 20.00.
847. Uncirculated. Almost a brilliant proof. Handsome specimen. 3.00.
848. Uncirculated. Mint bloom. 3.50.
849. Uncirculated. Mint bloom. 3.00.
850. *Brilliant proof.* 25.00.
851. *Brilliant proof.* 65.00.
852. Uncirculated. Brilliant mint lustre. 60.00.
853. Uncirculated. Brilliant mint lustre. 5.00.
854. *Brilliant proof.* 30 00.
855. *Brilliant proof.* 25.00.
856. Uncirculated. Brilliant mint bloom. Scarcely perceptible pin scratch in field. 3.50.
857. *Proof.* A few stars not sharp. 6.00.
858. *Brilliant proof.* 60.00.
859. O. Mint. Nearly uncirculated. Brilliant mint lustre. 2.00.
859. S. Mint. Barely circulated. Very rare. 7.50.
860. O. Mint. Uncirculated. Brilliant mint lustre. 3.00.
863. Dollar, half and quarter. With legend " In God we Trust " above eagle on reverse. Brilliant proofs. *Unique.* 125.00.

1864. Dollar, half and quarter. With legend " In God we Trust " above eagle on reverse. Brilliant proofs. Excessively rare. Only about 5 sets known. 50.00.
1865. Dollar, half and quarter. With legend " In God we Trust " above eagle on reverse. Brilliant proofs. Excessively rare. 40.00.
1891. O. Mint. Uncirculated. Mint bloom. 1.35.

United States Half Dollars.

1794. Barely circulated. Considerable lustre. One of the best of the date I have seen. 35.00.
1794. Very fine. Bold impression. Date strong. 8.00.
1795. Uncirculated. Mint lustre. Planchet file marks. 10.00.
1797. Very fine specimen of this rare date. 125.00.
1801. Extremely fine. Choice specimen. 15.00.
1802. Extremely fine. 15.00.
1803. *Italic 3.* Barely circulated. Hair lines sharp. A beauty. 3.00.
1805 over '04. Very fine. 7.50.
1806. *Proof.* 10.00.
1806. No stem in eagle's claw. Uncirculated. Brilliant mint bloom. 10.00.
1807. Head to right. Uncirculated. Brilliant mint bloom. 10.00.
1807. Head to left. About uncirculated. Sharp. 3.50.
1808. Perfect date. Uncirculated. Brilliant mint iustre. 4.00.
1809. Uncirculated. Brilliant mint bloom. Very sharp and handsome. 3.00.
1810. Uncirculated. Brilliant mint lustre. 3.00.
1811. Uncirculated. Brilliant mint lustre. 2.00.
1812. Uncirculated. Brilliant mint lustre. 2.00.
1813. Uncirculated. Brilliant mint lustre. Sharp. 2.00.
1814. Uncirculated. Brilliant mint lustre. 2.00.
1815. Uncirculated. Semi-proof. One of the handsomest specimens of this date known. 25.00.
1815. Uncirculated. Sharp. 15.00.
1817. Uncirculated. Mint bloom. 2.00.
1818. *Brilliant proof.* 15.00.
1818 over '17. Uncirculated. Mint bloom. 1.50.
1819. Uncirculated. Mint lustre. 1.50.
1819 over '18. Uncirculated. Mint bloom. 1.50.
1820. Large, wide date. Knobbed 2. Uncirculated. Mint bloom. 2.00.
1820. Large date, curled 2. Uncirculated. Mint bloom. 2.00.
1820. Small date. Uncirculated. Mint bloom. 2.00.
1820. Over '19. *Proof.* A beauty. 10.00.
1821. Uncirculated. Mint lustre. Sharp and handsome. 2.00.
1822. Uncirculated. Mint lustre. Sharp and handsome. 2.00.
1823. Uncirculated. Mint bloom. 1.50.
1824. Uncirculated. Mint lustre. Handsome. 1.50

1825. Uncirculated. Mint lustre. Handsome. 1.50.
1826. Uncirculated. Proof impression. 3.50.
1827. *Proof.* 5.00.
1828. Plain 2. Small date. Uncirculated. Mint bloom. Handsome. 1.50.
1828. Curled 2. *Proof.* 7.50.
1829. *Proof.* Splendid specimen. 7.50.
1830. *Brilliant proof.* 12.50.
1831. Uncirculated. Mint lustre. 1.00.
1832. Uncirculated. Mint lustre. 1.00.
1833. Uncirculated. Mint lustre. 1.00.
1834. Large date. *Brilliant proof.* 12.50.
1834. Small date. Uncirculated. Mint lustre. 1.00.
1835. Uncirculated. Mint lustre. 1.50.
1836. Uncirculated. Brilliant mint lustre. Sharp and handsome. 2.00.
1836. Milled edge. Brilliant proof, a little haymarked. 15.00.
1837. Uncirculated. Handsome mint bloom. 2 00.
1838. Uncirculated. Mint lustre. 1.50.
1839. Head. Uncirculated. Mint lustre. 1.50.
1839. O. Mint. (O under head). Uncirculated. Brilliant mint lustre. 2.50.
1839. Liberty seated. *With drapery from elbow to knee.* Uncirculated. 2.50.
1840. Uncirculated. Mint lustre. Very handsome specimen. 2.50.
1840. O. Mint. Small O. Uncirculated. Brilliant mint bloom. 2.50.
1841. O. Mint. Uncirculated. Sharp. Semi-proof. 2.50.
1842. Large date. Proof surface. Very handsome specimen. 3.00.
1842. Large date. O. Mint. Uncirculated. Brilliant mint lustre. 2.00.
1843. Uncirculated. Beautiful mint bloom. 2.00.
1843. O. Mint. Uncirculated. Mint lustre. 2.00.
1844. *Proof.* 4.00.
1844. O. Mint. Uncirculated. Mint lustre. Semi-proof. 3.00.
1845. Uncirculated. Mint bloom. 2.00.
1846. Yankee 6. Uncirculated. Mint bloom. Beautiful sharp specimen. 1.50.
1847. Uncirculated. Mint lustre. Beautiful sharp specimen. 2.00.
1847. O. Mint. Uncirculated. Mint lustre. Slight proof surface. 2.50.
1848. Uncirculated. Mint lustre. 2.00.
1849. *Brilliant proof.* 7.50.
1849. O. Mint. Uncirculated. Mint lustre. 2.00.
1851. O. Mint. Uncirculated. Mint lustre. 2.50.
1851. P. Mint. Uncirculated. Mint lustre. 2.50.
1852. P. Mint. Uncirculated. Mint lustre. 6.00.
1852. O. Mint. *Proof impression.* 7.50.

1854. *Brilliant proof.* 7.50.
1854. O. Mint. Uncirculated. Mint lustre. Semi-proof. 2.00.
1855. O. Mint. Uncirculated. Mint lustre. 1.50.
1856. O. Mint. Uncirculated. Mint lustre. 1.50.
1858. Uncirculated. Mint lustre. Handsome, sharp specimen. 1.25.

United States Quarters.

1796. *Sharp proof.* Beautiful specimen. 75.00.
1796. Extremely fine, barely circulated. 20.00.
1804. Quite fine. Unusually bold. 15.00.
1805. Very fine and bold. 3.00.
1806 The centre of obverse and corresponding portion of reverse a little weak from weak die, otherwise uncirculated, brilliant mint lustre. 7.50.
1806 over '05. Fine and bold. 1.50.
1807. But little circulated. Considerable lustre. 10.00.
1807. Fine and bold. 2.00.
1815. Small E above head. Uncirculated. Mint lustre. 3.00.
1818. Uncirculated. Mint lustre. 2.00.
1819. Barely circulated. Mint lustre. 2.00.
1820. Large O. *Proof.* 10.00.
1820. Small O. Semi-proof. Rare. 15.00.
1821. *Brilliant proof.* 7.50.
1821. Uncirculated. Mint lustre. 3.00.
1822. Uncirculated. Mint lustre. Handsome. 8.50.
1823. In good condition for this rare date, the date bold. 60.00.
1824. Quite fine. Rare so choice. 5.00.
1825. Uncirculated. Mint lustre. 3.00.
1827. *Brilliant proof.* 150.00.
1828. *Proof.* 7.50.
1828. Uncirculated. Semi-proof. 3.50.
1831. Uncirculated. Mint lustre. 1.00.
1833. Uncirculated. Mint bloom. Beautiful specimen. 3.00.
1834. Uncirculated. Mint lustre. 1.00.
1835. Uncirculated. Mint lustre. 1.00.
1837. *Proof.* 2.50.
1837. Uncirculated. Mint lustre. 1.50.
1839. Uncirculated. Mint bloom. 1.50.
1843. Uncirculated. Mint lustre. 1.25.
1845. Uncirculated. Mint lustre. A beauty. 1.50.
1846. *Brilliant proof.* 10.00.
1847. Uncirculated. Mint lustre. 1.50.
1849. *Brilliant proof.* 10.00.
1849. Uncirculated. Semi-proof. 1.50.
1850. Uncirculated. Semi-proof. 1.50.
1852. Uncirculated. Mint lustre. 2.00.
1853. *Without arrows or rays.* Uncirculated. Mint lustre. 15.00.
1856. *Brilliant proof.* 10.00.

1857. O. Mint. Uncirculated. Semi proof. Handsome. 2.00.
1858. Brilliant proof. 2.00.

United States Twenty Cents.

1875. Brilliant proof. 1.00.
1875. P. and S. Mints. Uncirculated. Mint bloom. Pair .75.
1876. Brilliant proof. 1.00.
1876. Uncirculated. Brilliant mint lustre. .50.
1877. Brilliant proof. 3.00.
1878. Brilliant proof. 2.50.

United States Dimes.

1796. Cracked die. Uncirculated. Brilliant. 15.00.
1796. Perfect die. Uncirculated. Brilliant mint lustre. Very sharp and handsome. 20.00.
1797. Thirteen stars. The hair lines but little worn. Extremely fine and best offered for some time. 25.00.
1797. Sixteen stars. Very fine, but centre of reverse scratched. 12.50.
1798 over '97. 15 stars above eagle's head on reverse. Very fine. 15.00.
1798 over '97. 13 stars above eagle's head on reverse. Very good. , Very rare variety. 10.00.
1798. Perfect date. Except the stars to left, which are a little worn, the piece is almost uncirculated. Nice specimen. 25.00.
1800. Could almost be called uncirculated. A beauty. 40.00.
1801. Very good, bold, clean impression. Fine for date. 7.50.
1802. But for the fact that this coin has been honey-stoned to clean corrosion (though this has been skillfully done), it would be a very fine specimen. It is still fine and desirable. 10.00.
1803. Extremely fine. In this condition exceedingly rare. 25.00.
1804. Barely touched by circulation. The hair lines bold and sharp. Excelled by few. 75.00.
1804. Quite fine and bold, nearly all the hair lines show. 35.00.
1805. Uncirculated. Brilliant mint lustre. 15.00.
1807. Barely touched. Brilliant mint lustre. 3 light scratches. 5.00.
1807. Beard variety. Uncirculated. Mint bloom. 10.00.
1809. Uncirculated. Brilliant mint lustre. 50.00.
1809. Quite fine and bold. 5.00.
1811. Quite fine and bold. 5.00.
1811. Over '09. Scarcely touched by circulation. A handsome piece. 20.00.
1814. *Large date.* Uncirculated. Brilliant mint lustre. 7.50.
1820. Uncirculated. Large 10 in 10 C. Mint lustre. 5.00.
1820. Uncirculated. Small 10 in 10 C. Mint lustre. 5.00.
1821. *Large date.* Uncirculated. Mint lustre. 3.00.
1821. *Small date.* Barely circulated. Mint bloom. 2.00.

1822. Very good. 2.50.
1823. Uncirculated. Mint lustre. 12.50.
1825. *Brilliant proof. Sharp and perfect.* 20.00.
1825. Uncirculated. Brilliant mint bloom. 5.00.
1827. Uncirculated. Brilliant mint bloom. 5.00.
1828. *Small date.* Uncirculated. Sharp. Brilliant mint lustre.
       Handsome specimen. 7.50.
1829. Uncirculated. Brilliant mint lustre. Very sharp and
       handsome. 2.50.
1830. *Brilliant proof.* 10.00.
1830. Uncirculated. Brilliant mint bloom. Handsome. 2.00.
1831. *Brilliant proof.* 10.00.
1832. *Proof.* Nick on edge. 2.00.
1833. Uncirculated. Mint lustre. 1.50.
1834. *Brilliant proof.* 10.00.
1835. *Brilliant proof.* 10.00.
1835. Uncirculated. Brilliant mint bloom. Handsome. 2.00.
1836. Uncirculated. Mint lustre. 1.00.
1837. Head. Uncirculated. Mint lustre. 1.50.
1837. Liberty seated. Large date. Sharp brilliant proof. 2.50.
1838. *Without stars.* Uncirculated. Mint lustre. 10.00.
1838. *With stars.* Uncirculated. A beauty. Mint lustre. 1.50.
1839. Uncirculated. Brilliant mint lustre. Sharp. 2.00.
1840. Without drapery. *Brilliant proof.* 5.00.
1841. Uncirculated. Mint lustre. 1.25.
1841. O. Mint. Uncirculated. Mint lustre. 1.50.
1842. Uncirculated. Mint lustre. ˙ 2.00.
1843. Uncirculated. Mint lustre. 1.25.
1845. Uncirculated. Mint lustre. 1.25.
1846. *Brilliant proof.* 15.00.
1848. Uncirculated. Mint lustre. 3.00.
1849. *Brilliant proof.* 10.00.
1850. Uncirculated. Mint lustre. 1.25.
1851. Uncirculated. Mint lustre. 1.25.
1852. *Brilliant proof.* 7.50.
1852. Uncirculated. Mint lustre. 1.00.
1853. *Without arrows.* Uncirculated. Mint lustre. 1.50.
1853. *With arrows.* *Proof.* 2.50.
1853. *With arrows.* Uncirculated. Mint lustre. .75.
1854. O. Mint. Uncirculated. .75.
1855   *Brilliant proof.* 7.50.
1856. *Large date.* Extremely fine. .75.
1856. *Small date.* Uncirculated. Mint lustre. 1.25.
1856. *Small date.* O. Mint. Uncirculated. Mint lustre. 1.25.
1857. Uncirculated. Mint lustre. .50.
1857. O. Mint. Uncirculated. Mint lustre. 1.00.
1858. *Brilliant proof.* 2.00.
1858. Uncirculated. Mint lustre. Sharp, handsome specimen. .75.

1859. O. Mint. Uncirculated. Mint lustre. 1.00.
1860. S. Mint. Uncirculated, brilliant mint lustre. Extremely rare in this condition. 15.00.

United States Half Dimes.

1794. Uncirculated with proof surface. A gem. 25.00.
1795. Uncirculated. Semi-proof. 12.50.
1796. Uncirculated. Brilliant mint lustre. Sharp impression. 35.00.
1796. Barely touched by circulation. Sharp and handsome. 20.00.
1797. *Thirteen stars.* Nick to left of date otherwise quite fine and bold. 3.50.
1797. *Fifteen stars.* Extremely fine. Sharp and handsome. 15.00.
1797. *Sixteen stars.* Uncirculated. Brilliant mint lustre. Sharp and handsome. 30.00.
1800. Very fine. 3.50.
1800. LIBEKTY. Very good and bold. 2.00.
1801. Shows but little circulation. One of the best of this date. 20.00.
1802. A good specimen of this extremely rare date. 100.00.
1803. Large 8. Quite fine. Nearly all the hair lines show. 10.00.
1805. Barest touch of circulation. Sharp and handsome. 35.00.
1829. Uncirculated. Mint lustre. .50.
1830. Uncirculated. Mint lustre. .50.
1831. *Brilliant proof.* 7.50.
1831. Uncirculated. .75.
1832. Uncirculated. Semi-proof. .75.
1832. Knobbed 8. Uncirculated. Mint lustre. .75.
1833. Uncirculated. Mint lustre. .75.
1834. *Brilliant proof.* 10.00
1834. Uncirculated. Mint lustre. .75.
1835. Large date. Uncirculated. Mint lustre. .75.
1835. Small date. Brilliant proof. 7.50.
1835. Small date. Uncirculated. Mint lustre. .50.
1836. Uncirculated. Mint lustre. .75.
1837. *Head.* Uncirculated. Mint lustre. .75.
1837. *No stars. Curved date. Brilliant proof.* 7.50.
1837. *No stars. Curved date.* Uncirculated. Mint bloom. Sharp. Beautiful specimen. 2.50.
1837. *No stars. Straight date.* Uncirculated. Mint bloom. 1.50.
1838. *No stars.* Uncirculated. Brilliant mint bloom. Extremely rare in this condition. 15.00.
1838. *With stars. Brilliant proof.* 7.50.
1838. *With stars.* Uncirculated. Mint lustre. 1.00.
1839. *Proof.* 2.50.
1840. *With drapery. Fine proof.* 5.00.

1840.   *Without drapery.* Uncirculated. Mint lustre. Semi-proof. 1.50.
1841.   *Brilliant proof.* 10.00.
1841.   Uncirculated. Mint lustre. 1.25.
1842.   *Brilliant proof.* 12.50.
1842.   Uncirculated. Mint lustre. Sharp. Slight proof surface. 3.50.
1843.   Uncirculated. Mint lustre. 1.00.
1844.   P. Mint. *Brilliant proof.* 10.00.
1844.   P. Mint. Uncirculated. Mint lustre. Some proof surface. A beauty. 3.50.
1845.   Uncirculated. Semi-proof. 2.00.
1846.   Very fine specimen, showing but little circulation. 7.50.
1847.   *Brilliant proof.* 12.50.
1847.   Uncirculated. Mint lustre. 1.00.
1848.   Large date. Uncirculated. Brilliant mint bloom. 12.50.
1848.   *Large date.* Very fine. Rare so choice. 5.00. ·
1848.   *Small date.* Obverse brilliant proof; rev., mint bloom. A beauty. 10.00.
1849.   *Brilliant proof.* 10.00.
1849.   Uncirculated. Mint lustre. Some proof surface. 1.50.
1850.   Uncirculated. Mint lustre. Sharp and handsome. 1.00
1851.   Uncirculated. Proof surface. 1.00.
1851.   O. Mint. Uncirculated. Mint lustre. 1.00.
1852.   Uncirculated. Mint bloom. A sharp little beauty. 1.00.
1852.   *Brilliant proof.* 7.50.
1853.   *Without arrows.* Almost a brilliant proof. Handsome. 3.00.
1853.   *With arrows.* Proof surface. 1.00.
1854.   *Brilliant proof.* 7.50.
1854.   Uncirculated. Mint lustre. .50.
1855.   *Brilliant proof.* 7.50.
1855.   Uncirculated. Mint lustre. .50.
1856.   *Brilliant proof.* 5.00.
1857.   Uncirculated. Mint bloom. .50.
1857.   O. Mint. *Brilliant proof.* 7.50.
1857.   O. Mint. Uncirculated. Mint lustre. 1.00.
1858.   *Brilliant proof.* 2.00.
1859.   O. Mint. Uncirculated. Mint lustre. .50.
1860.   *With stars. Proof.* 7.50.
1860.   O. Mint. Uncirculated. Mint lustre. .75.

United States Silver Three Cents.

1851.   Uncirculated. Mint lustre. Proof surface. 2.00.
1851.   Uncirculated. Mint lustre. .50.
1851.   O. Mint. Uncirculated. Mint lustre. .75.
1852.   Uncirculated. Mint lustre. .50.
1853.   Uncirculated. Mint lustre. .35.
1854.   *Brilliant proof.* 7.50.
1854.   Uncirculated. Mint lustre. 1.50.

1855. *Brilliant proof.* 7.50.
1855. Uncirculated. Mint lustre. 2.00.
1856. Uncirculated. Mint lustre. 1.50.
1857. Uncirculated. Mint lustre. .50.
1858. Brilliant proof. 2.00.
1858. Uncirculated. Mint lustre. .50.
1859. Brilliant proof. .75.
1860. Brilliant proof. .75.
1861. Brilliant proof. .75.
1862. Brilliant proof. .50.
1863. Uncirculated. Mint bloom. Rarer than proof. 1.00.
1864. Uncirculated. Mint bloom. Rarer than proof. 2.00.
1865. Uncirculated. Mint bloom. Rarer than proof. 1.50.
1866. Brilliant proof. 1.00.
1867. Brilliant proof. 1.00.
1868. Brilliant proof. 1.00.
1869. Brilliant proof. 1.50.
1870. Dull proof. .75.
1871. Uncirculated. Mint lustre. Semi-proof. 75.
1872. Brilliant proof. .75.
1873. Brilliant proof. 1.00.

United States Minor Coinage.

1856. Nickel Cent. Brilliant proof. 6.00.
1858. Nickel Cents. Large and small letters in legends. Brilliant proofs. Pair 2.00.
1859. Nickel Cent. Brilliant proof. .50.
1860. Nickel Cent. Brilliant proof. .75.
1861. Nickel Cent. Brilliant proof. 1.00.
1862. Nickel Cent. Brilliant proof. .40.
1863. Nickel Cent. Brilliant proof. .40.
1864. Nickel Cent. Brilliant proof. .75.
1865. Bronze Cent. Brilliant proof. .50.
1869. Two Cents. Brilliant proof. .50.
1865. Five Cents. *Without rays. Of this date only two specimens are known, and I own both.* Brilliant proof. 15.00.
1866. Five Cents. *With rays.* Brilliant proof. .50.
1866. Five Cents. *Without rays. Brilliant proof.* Extremely rare. 5.00.
1877. Five Cents. Brilliant proof. 2.00.
1873. Minor proof set. 1, 2, 3, 5 cents. 1.75.
1877. Minor proof set. 1, 3, 5 cents. 4.00.
1878. Minor proof set. 1, 3, 5 cents. .75.

United States Cents.

1793. Chain "America." No periods after "Liberty" and date. The masses of hair slightly worn, otherwise about uncirculated. Light olive. 50.00.

1793. Chain "America." Periods after "Liberty" and date. Nearly uncirculated. Brown. 25.00.
1793. Wreath. Broad head and leaves. Small date. Very fine specimen. 12.50.
1793. Wreath. Stem of leaves over 7 and 9 of date. Very fine. Light color. 15.00.
1793. Wreath. Stem above 9 of date. Lettered edge. Fine. Light brown. 10.00.
1793. Wreath. Stem above 9 of date. Vine and bars on edge (not often found on this variety). Very fine. Light brown with traces of original red. 15.00.
1793. Liberty Cap. Very good. Beaded milling complete on both sides. Steel color. 12.50.
1794. Maris No. 1. "1793 Head." Fair. 1.00.
1794. Maris No. 2. " Double Chin." Good. 1.50.
1794. Maris No. 3. " Sans Milling." Fine. Brown. 2.00.
1794. Maris No. 5. " Young Head." Before obverse die cracked. But little circulated. Beautiful olive green. 10.00.
1794. Maris No. 9. " Crooked 7." Barely circulated, hair sharp. Light brown. 12.50.
1794. Maris No. 11. " Many Haired." Good. 1.00.
1794. Maris No. 12. " Scarred Head." Extremely fine. Light olive. 12.50.
1794. Maris No. 13. " Standless 4." Very fine. Brown. 3.50.
1794. Maris No. 14. " Abrupt Hair." Only touched on the masses of hair. Light olive. 12.50.
1794. Maris No. 17. " The Ornate." Very fine. Brown. 4.00.
1794. Maris No. 20. " Fallen 4." Very fine. Brown. 4.00.
1794. Maris No. 21. " Short Bust." Very good. 1.00.
1794. Maris No. 24. " Patagonian." Fine. Brown. 2.00.
1794. Maris No. 25. " The Ornate." Very fine. Steel color. 3.50.
1794. Maris No. 26. " Amiable Face." Very fine. Light brown. 3.50.
1794. Maris No. 27. "Amiable Face." Fair. 1.00.
1794. Maris No. 28. " Large Planchet." Very good. Brown. 1.00.
1794. Maris No. 29. " Marred Field." Fine. Light olive. 2.50.
1794. Maris No. 32. " Shielded Hair." About fine. Brown. 2.00.
1794. Maris No. 36. " The Plicæ." Nearly fine. Brown. 2.00.
1794. Maris No. 38. " Roman Plicæ." Fine. Light brown. 2.50.
1794. Maris No. 39. " 1795 Head." Quite fine. Dark olive. 3.50.
1794. Maris No. 42. "Trephined Head." About fine. 2.00.
1794. Maris No. 46. Very fine. Hair but little worn. 5.00.
1794. Maris No. 50. Fine. 3.00.
1795. Lettered edge. Uncirculated. Beautiful light olive. In this condition excessively rare. 100.00.
1795. Lettered Edge. Fractional mark irregular. Berry on left of ribbon bow, none on right. Extremely fine. Brown. 20.00.

1795. Thick planchet, but unlettered edge. Barely circulated. Brown. 10.00.
1795. Thin Planchet, "One Cent" in center of wreath. Uncirculated. Beautiful glossy light olive. A splendid cent. 35.00.
1795 Thin Planchet. "One Cent" high in wreath. Uncirculated. Light olive with traces of original red. A few letters are a little weakly struck, otherwise a splendid specimen. 20.00.
1796. Liberty Cap. Wide date Very fine. 7.50.
1796. Fillet Head. Uncirculated. Brown. 20.00.
1796. Fillet Head. Broken die. Very fine. Steel color 5.00.
1797. Uncirculated. Red. 20.00.
1797. Break in die back of head near ribbon bow. Uncirculated. Brown. 15.00.
1797. Break in die back of head near bottom of hair. Uncirculated. Brown. 15.00.
1798. Large date. Extremely fine. Brown. 5.00.
1798. Small date. Extremely fine. Light olive. 5.00.
1799. Fine for date. The date particularly fine and well struck. Desirable specimen. 35.00.
1799 over '98. Quite fine Steel color. 30.00.
1800 over '99. Extremely fine. Hair lines scarcely touched. Good color. 5.00.
1800. Perfect date. Broken die. Extremely fine. Brown. 5.00.
1801. Weak impression but nearly uncirculated. Light olive. 3.50.
1801. 1-000, United and only one stem to wreath. Scarcely circulated. Light olive. Damaged by a dent near L and a scratch diagonally across head. 10.00.
1802. Uncirculated. Beautiful glossy light olive. Exceptionally · sharp and one of the very best of this date. 7.50.
1802. Uncirculated or barest touch. Glossy light brown. 3.50.
1802. No stems to wreath. Very fine. Brown. 3.00.
1802. Die broken below date. Barely touched. Handsome olive. 3.00.
1803. Small 1-100. Uncirculated. Light olive. 5.00.
1803. Die broken below date. But little circulated. Brown. 2.00.
1803. Large 3. But little circulated, very sharp Nice steel color. 6.00.
1804. Broken die. Fine. 15.00.
1804. Perfect die. Very good. Brown. 12.50.
1805. Scarcely circulated. Glossy light brown. 12.50.
1806. But little circulated. Steel color. 15.00.
1807. Perfect date. About uncirculated. Handsome purple brown. 7.50.
1807. Perfect date. Comet variety. Very fine. Light olive. 5.00.
1807 over '06. Fine. Light olive. 4.00.

1808. Scarcely circulated, but a light impression. Light olive.
10.00.
1808. 12 star variety (so-called). Very fine and sharp. Brown.
5.00.
1809. Uncirculated. Olive. 25.00.
1810. Perfect date. Barely circulated. Steel color. 7.50.
1810 over '09. Extremely fine. Glossy chocolate color. 5.00.
1811. Perfect date. Very nearly uncirculated. Glossy brown.
15.00.
1811 over '10. Very fine. Brown. 7.50.
1812. Large date. Uncirculated. Light olive. 20.00.
1812. Small date. Barely circulated. Light brown. 7.50.
1813. Uncirculated. Brown. 7.50.
1814. Plain 4. Double Chin. Uncirculated, or scarcely touched.
Light olive, but reverse stained slightly with green. 5.00.
1814. Cross 4. Uncirculated. Unusually sharp. Glossy chocolate color. 7.50.
1816. Perfect die. Uncirculated. Brilliant red. 3.00.
1816. Broken die. Uncirculated. Brilliant red. 2.00.
1817. Point of tiara between stars, wide date. Uncirculated.
Bright red. 1.50.
1817. Star near point of tiara. Uncirculated. Brilliant red. 2.50.
1817. The top-knot variety. Barely circulated. Glossy light
olive. 2.00.
1817. Fifteen stars. Extremely fine. Glossy light brown. 3.00.
1818. Uncirculated. Brilliant red. .50.
1819. Small date. Uncirculated. Brilliant red. Very sharp,
semi-proof impression. 3.00.
1819 over '18. Uncirculated. Partly bright. A few stars weak,
and spot of discoloration on reverse. 1.00.
1820. Perfect date. 2 with large curl. Uncirculated. Brilliant
red. 3.00.
1820. Uncirculated. Brilliant red. 1.00.
1820 over '19. Uncirculated. Beautiful light olive with traces
of original red. 6.00.
1821. Not much circulated. Glossy steel color. 7.50.
1822. Uncirculated or barely touched. Glossy light olive. 7.50.
1823 over '22. Quite fine. Olive. 7.50.
1823. Perfect date. Nearly fine. 2.00.
1824. Fine, but edge nicked. Brown. 1.50.
1825. Sharp, perfect, beautiful impression. Uncirculated. Handsome even reddish olive. 20.00.
1826. Uncirculated. Beautiful light olive. 15.00.
1827. Uncirculated. Light olive and partly bright. 15.00.
1828. Large date. Barely circulated. Very light olive. 7.50.
1828. Small date. Fine. Light brown. 3.00.
1829. Uncirculated. Handsome glossy olive-brown. 15.00.
1830. Small date. Sharp impression, sharp milling. Barely circulated. Beautiful purple color. 5.00.

1830. Large date. Barely circulated. Orange color. 5.00.
1831. Large letters in legend. Uncirculated. Brilliant red. 10.00.
1831. Small letters in legend. Uncirculated. Beautiful light olive. 5.00.
1832. Uncirculated. Reddish olive. 10.00.
1833. Date near milling. Uncirculated. Brilliant red. 10.00.
1833. Date near head. Barely circulated. Light olive. 3.50.
1834. Small date. Uncirculated. Handsome light olive. 5.00.
1835. Barely circulated. Handsome light olive. 5.00.
1835. Large date. Very fine. Light brown. 4.00.
1836. Perfect die. But little circulated. Light olive. 3.00.
1836. Die broken to left. Uncirculated. Glossy reddish brown. 5.00.
1836. Die broken to right. Uncirculated. Brown. 5.00.
1837. Beaded hair-string. Small letters on reverse. Proof. 12.50.
1837. Plain hair-string. Uncirculated. Brilliant red. 3.00.
1838. *Brilliant proof.* 12.50.
1838. Uncirculated. Brilliant red. 3.00.
1839. Head of 1838. Barely circulated. Greenish-olive. 3.00.
1839. Booby Head. Uncirculated. Glossy light olive. 5.00.
1839. Silly Head. Very fine. Steel-brown. 2.00.
1839. Head of 1840. Extremely fine. Light brown with traces of red. 3.00.
1839 over '36. Very good. Better than usually found. 4.00.
1840. Large date. Uncirculated. Almost a brilliant proof. Glossy olive. 5.00.
1840. Small date. Barest touch of circulation. Glossy light olive. 3.00.
1840. Small date. Doubly cut date. Barely circulated. Glossy light brown. 3.00.
1841. *Brilliant proof.* 20.00.
1842. Large date. Uncirculated. Light olive. 2.00.
1842. Small date. Extremely fine. Light brown. 2.00.
1843. Obverse and reverse of 1842. *Brilliant proof.* 20.00.
1843. Obverse and reverse of 1842. Uncirculated. Brilliant red. 10.00.
1843. Obverse and reverse of 1844. Uncirculated. Light brown. 5.00.
1844. *Brilliant proof.* 20.00.
1844. Barely circulated. Light olive. 2.00.
1845. Uncirculated. Purple red. 2.00.
1846. Dutch 6. Uncirculated. Glossy brown. Handsome sur-surface, nearly proof. 4.00.
1847. *Brilliant proof.* 20.00.
1847. Uncirculated. Brilliant red. 3.00.
1848. *Brilliant proof.* 20.00.
1849. *Brilliant proof.* 15.00.
1849. Uncirculated. Brilliant red. 2.00.

1850. *Brilliant proof.* 12.50.
1850. Uncirculated. Brilliant red. Beautiful specimen. Semi-proof. 1.50.
1851. Uncirculated. Brilliant red. Beautiful clean specimen. 1.00.
1852. Uncirculated. Brilliant red. Beautiful clean sharp specimen, with some proof surface. 1.50.
1853. Uncirculated. Brilliant red. Clean specimen. .75.
1854. Uncirculated. Brilliant red. Clean specimen. 1.00.
1855. Slanting 5's. *Brilliant proof.* 7.50.
1855. Straight 5's. Uncirculated. Brilliant red. Nice specimen. .75.
1856. Slanting 5. Uncirculated. Brilliant red. .50.
1856. Straight 5. Uncirculated. Brilliant red. .75.
1857. Small date. Uncirculated. Light olive. .75.
1857. Large date. Uncirculated. Light olive. 1.00.

United States Half Cents.

1793. Uncirculated. Glossy brown. 15.00.
1794. Date close to bust. Uncirculated. Glossy steel color. 10.00.
1794. Date distant from bust. Uncirculated. Glossy light olive. 15.00.
1795. Lettered edge. About uncirculated. Light olive. 12.50.
1795. Thin planchet. Uncirculated. Handsome surface. 15.00.
1797. Date close to head. About uncirculated. 6.00.
1797. Date distant from head. Fine. Brown. Broad milling. 3.00.
1802. Quite fine and bold. Rare in this condition. 7.50.
1806. Large date. Uncirculated. Brilliant red. 1.50.
1806. Small date. No stems to wreath. Extremely fine. Light olive. 1.50.
1809. Uncirculated. Handsome color. 2.50.
1810. Very fine. Brown. 1.50.
1811. Fine and bold. 3.00.
1825. Uncirculated. Reddish-purple. 1.50.
1826. Uncirculated. Beautiful light olive. 1.50.
1828. 12 stars. Uncirculated. Glossy light olive. 1.50.
1828. 13 stars. Uncirculated. Brilliant red. .75.
1832. Uncirculated. Glossy light olive. 1.00.
1833. *Brilliant proof.* 5.00.
1834. *Proof.* 3.50.
1834. Uncirculated. Beautiful light olive. Sharp. A gem. 1.50.
1835. Semi-proof. Brilliant red. 2.50.
1841. Large berries on reverse. *Brilliant proof.* 17.50.
1848. Large berries on reverse. *Brilliant proof.* 20.00.
1849. Uncirculated. Glossy light olive. 1.00.
1850. *Brilliant proof.* 5.00.
1851. Uncirculated. Mint lustre. .75.

1852. *Brilliant proof.* 12.50.
1853. Uncirculated. Mint lustre. .75.
1854. Uncirculated. Mint lustre. .75.
1855. *Brilliant proof.* 3.50.
1855. Uncirculated. Mint lustre. .50.
1856. *Brilliant proof.* 3.50.
1857. *Brilliant proof.* 3.50.
1857. Uncirculated. Mint lustre. .50.

Washington Coins.

1783. " Unity States" Cent. Very fine. Light olive. .75.
1783. Small head. " United States" Cent. Very fine. Brown. 1.00.
1783. Small head. "United States" Cent. *Engrilled edge.* Very rare variety. Very fine. 2.50.
Double-head Cent. Uncirculated. Glossy light brown. 2.50.
1791. Cent. Large eagle. *Brilliant proof.* 6.00.
1791. Cent. Small eagle. Very fine. 5.00.
1792. Silver Half Dollar. " G. Washington President I. 1792." Very good specimen of this rare coin, but a small hole above head has been skillfully plugged. 50.00.
1792. Cent. Very good. Brown. 12.50.
1792. Cent. " Washington President 1792." The rare variety with one star above eagle's head. Extra fine, light brown color. Marred a little by several nicks on obverse. 40.00.
1793. Half-penny, rev., ship. Extra fine. Olive brown. 3.00.
Liberty and Security. Large size. Edge lettered : " An asylum for the oppress'd of all nations." Uncirculated. Bright. 3.50.
Liberty and Security. Small size. About uncirculated. Glossy brown. 2.50.
North Wales Token. Fine for piece. 1.50.
1795. Grate Cent. Nearly uncirculated. 2.00.
Success to U. S. Large and small sizes. Barely circulated. Nice pair. 2.50.
Funeral Medal. Reverse, skull and cross-bones. Pierced at top as usual. Silver. Good. Size 18. Rare. 5.00.

American Colonials.

SILVER.

1783. Chalmers Annapolis Shilling. Extremely fine. 12.50.
1783. Chalmers Annapolis Sixpence. Fine. 15.00.
1783. Chalmers Annapolis Threepence. Extremely fine. A little beauty. 17.50.
1652. Massachusetts Pine Tree Shilling. Small planchet. Fine. 6.50.
1652. Mass. Oak Tree Threepence. Crosby 5 B. Fine. Struck on an unusually large planchet making it sixpence size. 10.00.

1652.   Mass. Pine Tree Threepence. Very fair or good. 3.00.
1662.   Mass. Oak Tree Twopence. Fine. 5.00.

COPPER.

1722.   Rosa Americana Twopence. Good. 2.00.
1722.   Rosa Americana Penny. Plain rose. Uncirculated. 5.00.
1722.   Rosa Americana Half-penny. Very fine. 2.50.
1723.   Rosa Americana Penny. Crowned rose. Extremely fine.
        3.00.
1722.   Louisiana Cent. Good. 1.00.
1767.   Louisiana Cent. R. F. Fine. Brown. 1.00.
1766.   Pitt Token. "No stamps." About uncirculated. Glossy
        light olive. A beauty. 5.00.
1766.   Pitt Token. Same as last, but appears to have been struck
        in pewter or a composition containing a considerable
        portion of that metal. About uncirculated. 5.00.
1785.   Vermonts Res Publica. Very good. 2.00.
1786.   Vermontensium. Very fine. Light brown. 3.00.
1786.   Auctori Vermon. Baby head. Fine for piece. 3 00.
1785.   Vermon Auctori. Rev., "Immune Columbia." Always
        poor—this about as usually found. 5.00.
1787.   Massachusetts Cent. Horned eagle. Extremely fine. Olive
        color. 2.50.
1787.   Massachusetts Half Cent. Uncirculated. Light olive. 3.50.
1788.   Massachusetts Half Cent. Uncirculated. Partly bright.
        3.50.
1787.   Connecticut Cent. Horned Bust. Very fine. 1.00.
1787.   Connecticut Cent. "Auctori Connect." Last part of
        "Auctori" and corresponding reverse weak, otherwise
        uncirculated. Light brown. 1.00.
1786.   Auctori Plebis. Plain bust. I. C. under head. Rev.,
        "Hispanola." Large legends. Very good. Rare. 1.50.
1786.   Auctori Plebis. Draped bust. Rev., "Hispanola." Small
        legends. Fine. Light color. 2.00.
1786.   Auctori Plebis. Draped bust. Larger legend. Reverse
        seems to be plain or extremely weakly struck. Fine. 1.50.
1776.   Continental Currency. Tin Dollar. 2 R's in "Currency."
        Very fine 10.00.
1776.   Continental Currency. Tin Dollar. The rare variety with
        only one R in "Currency." Extremely fine. 12.50.
1787.   New York Cent. "Liber Natus Libertatem Defendo."
        Indian with tomahawk and bow. Rev., Arms of New
        York, "Excelsior" below. Very good or fine excepting
        that a small hole at Indian's feet has been plugged. Ex-
        tremely rare. 25.00.
1787.   New York Cent. Arms of New York, "Excelsior" below;
        rev., eagle. Very good. 20.00.
1787.   Nova Eborac. Seated figure to right. Very fine. Light
        brown. 4.00.

1787. Nova Eborac. Seated figure to left. Fine. 3.00.
1787. Nova Eborac. The extremely rare variety with two quatre-foils before " Nova." Nearly fine. Light brown. 10.00.
1794. Talbot, Allum & Lee. John Howard reverse. Very fine. Brown. 1.50.
1795. Talbot, Allum & Lee. Uncirculated. Light olive. 2.00.
Kentucky Cent. Thin planchet. Uncirculated. 2.00.
Kentucky Cent. Lettered edge. Uncirculated. Glossy olive. Semi-proof surface. 3.00.
1787. Immunis Columbia. Liberty seated on globe. Fine. Light color. 6.00.
1787. Franklin Cent. "Mind your business." Rev., "States United." Uncirculated. Bright red. .75.
1787. Franklin Cent. Same, but reverse, " United States." Un-circulated. Bright red. Planchet a little defective. Rare. 1.25.
1788. New Jersey. Fox type. Small horse on reverse. Very good. 1.00.
1788. New Jersey. Horse head to left. Very good. 1.50.
New Jersey. St. Patrick Halfpenny (" Mark Newby "). St. Pat-rick showing shamrock to people. Good. 1.50.
New Jersey. St. Patrick Farthing. St. Patrick banishing the snakes from Ireland. Very fine. 2.00.
1773. Virginia Half Cent. Uncirculated. Brilliant red. .75.
North Carolina Token (so-called). Ship; rev., shield, 13 stars. Brass. Uncirculated. 1.25.
1783. Nova Constellatio. Almost uncirculated. 1.00.
1783. Nova Constelatio (sic). Club rays. Extremely fine. Brown. 1.00.
1785. Nova Constellatio. Very fine. Olive color. 1.00.
James II. Tin Plantation Piece. Extremely fine. 2.00.
1778. Rhode Island piece. Ship. " De Admiraals flag van Ad-miraal Howe." Rev., 19 men marching on island; three ships. 13 boats. " Divlugtende Americaanen van Rohde Yland, Aug't, 1778." Brass. Uncirculated. 3.00.

United States Patterns.

1792. Martha Washington Half Disme. Very fine. 15.00.
1792. Silver-Centre Cent. Head of Liberty facing to right. LIBERTY PARENT OF SCIENCE & INDUSTRY. Rev., ONE CENT in wreath, $\frac{1}{100}$ below. UNITED STATES OF AMERICA. This specimen is struck on a full copper planchet—no hole for silver centre—and is rarer than the silver centre specimens. I know of no duplicate. Barely circulated. Dark olive. 100.00.
1838. Half Dollar. Liberty seated. Rev., flying eagle. Silver proof. 25.00.
1838. Half Dollar. Liberty seated. Rev., standing eagle. Silver proof. 25.00.

1838. Half Dollar. Head of Liberty. Rev., flying eagle. Silver, nearly proof. 4.00.
1838. Half Dollar. Head of Liberty. Rev., standing eagle. Silver proof. 7.50.
1839. Half Dollar. Nude bust of Liberty facing to *right*. Reverse same as regular issue of 1839–1841. Silver proof. 35.00.
1839. Half Dollar. Same as last, but with reverse of 1812–1865. Silver proof. 35.00.
1839. Half Dollar. Same as last. Copper proof. 5.00.
1849. Three Cents. Obv., same as ½ Dime. Silver proof. 5.00.
———. Three Cents. Large 3 ; rev., III. Nickel proof. 1.00.
1850. Three Cents. Liberty cap in rays. Brilliant proof. 3.50.
1850. Ring Cent. No hole ; rev., blank. Silver alloy. .75.
1853. Cent. Liberty head. Nickel. Dull proof. 1.00.
———. Blank obverse. Reverse same as last. Nickel proof. .50.
1854. Cent. Head of Liberty without stars. Bronze proof, 1.00.
1857. Cent. Head of Liberty ; rev., "One Cent" in wreath. Nickel proof. 3.00.
1858. Half Dollar. Obverse of regular issue. Reverse, Paquette's design with motto-ribbon in eagle's beak. Silver. Dull proof. 20.00.
1858. Quarter Dollar. Obverse of regular issue. Reverse, Paquette's design—no ribbon. Silver proof. 15.00.
1858. Cents. Set of twelve patterns. Indian head, large and small eagles, each with four reverses. 10.00.
1858. Cent. Indian head. Nickel proof. 1.00.
1859. Liberty Head. Reverses, "½ dollar," "Half dollar," "50 cents"—also, Liberty seated. Silver proofs. Set of 4 pieces for 6.00.
1859. Quarter Dollar. Obverse of regular issue. Reverse, Paquette's design—no motto-ribbon. Silver proof. 7.50.
1859. Cent. Regular issue ; rev., oak wreath and shield. Uncirculated. 1.00.
1861. Half Dollar. Rev's., "God our Trust" in field above eagle on reverse, and "God our Trust" on label. Brilliant proofs. Pair for 7.50.
1862. Half Dollar. Rev.'s., "God our Trust" in field above eagle on reverse, and "God our Trust" on label. Brilliant proofs. Pair for 5.00.
1863. Half Dollar. Rev's., "God our Trust" in field above eagle on reverse, and "God our Trust" on label. Brilliant proofs. Pair for 7.50.
1863. Pattern Three Cents. Obverse same as old copper cent; rev., "3 cents" in wreath. Copper proof. 2.50.
1863. Pattern Three Cents. Same as last. Aluminum proof. 5.00.
1863. Pattern Two Cents. Head of Washington. Rev., similar to regular issue, but "Cents" more curved. Aluminum proof. 3.00.

1863. Pattern Two Cents. Same as last, but thinner planchet. Aluminum proof. 3.00.

1863. Pattern Two Cents. Same as last. Nickel proof. 3.00.

1863. Pattern Two Cents. Same as last. Copper proof. 1.50.

1863. Pattern Two Cents. Similar to issue of 1864, but with reverse like last, " Cents" curved. Copper proof. 1.50.

1863. Pattern Two Cents. Same as last, but thin planchet. Copper proof. 1.50.

1863. Pattern Two Cents. Same as last. Nickel proof. 3.00.

1863. Cent. Thin planchet. Copper proof. 1.00.

1864. Quarter Dollar. Obverse of regular issue. Rev., smaller eagle with long arrows. Silver proof. 7.50.

1864. Cent. Obverse of regular type; reverse is obverse of 1858 eagle cent, small legend. Nickel proof. 5.00.

1865. Quarter Dollar. Obverse of regular issue. Rev., smaller eagle with long arrows. Silver proof. 7.50.

1865. Five Cents. Type adopted in 1867—no bars. Nickel proof. Extremely rare. 15.00.

1866. Five Cents. Head of Lineoln. Rev., Value in wreath. Nickel proof. 20.00.

1866. Five Cents. Head of Lincoln. Copper proof. 10.00.

1866. Five Cents. Head of Washington, "In God we Trust." Rev., 5 in wreath. Nickel proof. 1.50.

1866. Five Cents. Obv., same as last ; rev., same as regular issue. Nickel proof. 1.50.

1866. Five Cents. Obverse same as regular issue. Reverse, large 5 in wreath. Nickel proof. 1.50.

1866. Five Cents. Same as last, but small 5 in wreath. Nickel proof. 1.50.

1866. Five Cents. Obverse same as regular issue except that the date is separated by a boll ; reverse, 5 in wreath. Nickel proof. 1.50.

1867. Five Cents. Head of Liberty. Rev., " 5 cents" in wreath, " Cents" straight. Nickel proof. .75.

1867. Five Cents. Same as last, but "Cents " curved. Nickel proof. .75.

1867. Five Cents. Same as last, but the reverse is the regular issue without bars. Nickel proof. 10.00.

1867. Cent. Pure nickel. Uncirculated. 1.50.

1867. Five Cents. Longacre's design. Profile to left with long plumes. Rev., V. on shield. Aluminum proof. Rare. 1.50.

1868. Franco American Five Dollars. Obv., head to left ; rev., " 5 Dollars 25 Francs." Copper and aluminum proofs. Pair 5.00.

1868. Ten Cents. Obverse same as old copper cent. Nickel proof. 5.00.

1868. Ten Cents. Same as last. Copper proof. 2.50.

1868. Dime. Large star above and date below " One Dime " on reverse. Silver proof. 2.50.

1868. One, Three, Five Cents. Liberty head. Nickel proofs. 2.00.
1869. 50, 25, and 10 Cents. Draped head of Liberty, with Phrygian cap; another bust with plain diadem; another with star on forehead. Three of each value. Reeded edges. Silver proofs. Set of 9 pieces. 7.50.
1869. Similar set. Aluminum proofs. 5.00.
1869. Dimes. " Sil. 6, Nic. 1," and " Sil., Nic., Cop." Proofs. Pair 2.00.
1869. Five Cents. Large V on shield. Nickel proof: 1.50.
1869. Three Cents. Nickel. Dull proof. .50.
1870. 50, 25, and 10 Cents. Draped head of Liberty, with Phrygian cap; another bust with plain diadem; another with star on forehead. Three of each value. " Standard " in small letters on reverse. Reeded edges. Silver proofs. Set of 9 pieces. 7.50.
1870. Similar set. Aluminum proofs. 5.00.
1870. Similar set but " Standard Silver " in large letters. Silver proofs. 10.00.
1870. Similar to last. Aluminum proofs. 7.50.
1870. Longacre's Dollar. Indian queen. Silver proof. 20.00.
1870. Same. Aluminum proof. 5.00.
1870. Same. Copper proof. 2.50.
1870. Barber's beautiful patterns. Liberty seated with shield, and pole with cap. Values on reverse in figures within a wreath of cotton, corn and sugar. " Standard" above. Plain edges. $1, 50c., 25c., 10c., 5c. Silver proofs. Set for 40.00.   •
1870. Same. Reeded edges. Aluminum proofs. 15.00.
1870. Same. Reeded edge except the 5 and 10 cents. Copper proofs. 7.50.
1870. Same. Plain edges. Copper proofs. 7.50.
1870. Same, including a 3 cent piece. Reverse same as the regular issue. Reeded edges. Copper proofs. 7.50.
1870. Same as last. Dollar, half, quarter, dime and half-dime. Plain edges. Silver proofs. Set for 30.00.
1870. Same as last. Dollar, half, quarter and dime. All plain edges. Copper proofs. 5.00.
1871. Longacre's dollar, half, quarter, dime and half dime. Indian queen. Rev., 1 Dollar, etc., " Standard" above. Silver proofs. The dollar excessively rare. Set 50.00.
1871. Longacre's Indian Queen Dollar. Rev., same as regular issue. Silver proof. 25.00.
1871. Same. Aluminum proof. 7.50. Copper proof. 5.00.
1871. Same but no stars. Copper proof. Unique. 25.00.
1871. Five Cents. Head of Liberty. Rev., " 5 Cents " in wreath. Nickel proof. 2.00.
1871. Five Cents. Head of Liberty. Rev., " V Cents " in wreath. Nickel proof. 2.00.

1872. Barber's $1, 50 cts., 25 cts. Amazonian figure of Liberty seated caressing an eagle. Silver proofs. Set 50.00.

1873. Set of the six rare pattern Trade Dollars. Splendid proofs. 30.00.

1873. Trade Dollar. Profile with coronet. *Plain edge.* Silver proof. 10.00.

1873. Trade Dollar. The rare pattern with long plow handles. Silver proof. 25.00.

1874. International Coinage. Head of Liberty, " United States of America " above. Rev.. " 16.72 Grams. 900 Fine. Ubique." surrounded by labels " 10 Dollars," " Sterling £2. 1. 1.," etc. Copper proof. Rare. 5.00.

1874. Twenty Cents. Female seated on globe. Silver proof. 20.00.

1874. Twenty Cents. Female seated on globe. Copper proof. 5.00.

1875. Twenty Cents. Female seated on globe, holds olive branch, steamship at sea. Silver proof. 12.50.

1875. Twenty Cents. Head of Liberty ; reverse, " 20 " on shield. Silver proof. 12.50.

1875. Twenty Cents. Same as regular issue, but with reverse " ⅕ of a dollar." Silver proof. 12.50.

1877. Half Dollars. Head of Liberty in circle of pellets, " E Plurius Unum " above, date below, 7 stars to right, 6 to left. Reverses of Maris sale, Nos. 198, 199, 200. Copper proofs. 3 pcs. 7.50.

1877. Half Dollar. Head of Liberty with broad band inscribed " Liberty." 13 stars. Rev., Maris sale No. 204. Small eagle on large shield. Copper proof. 2.50.

1878. Goloid Metric Dollar. Brilliant proof. 10.00.

1878. Barber's beautiful pattern for the Standard Dollar. The rejected design, which was handsomer than the one by Morgan accepted. Also, the original Morgan design with only 3 leaves to branch under eagle's feet. Brilliant proofs. Pair for 15.00.

1879. Double Eagle. Has " 30 G. 1.5 S. 3.5 C. 35 grams 1879," separated by stars on obverse around Liberty head ; rev., same as regular issue. Gold proof. Only 3 struck. 100.00.

1879. Dollar. Obv., same as regular issue. Rev., a fine spread eagle, with drooping wings, holds arrows and branch. Silver proof. 35.00.

1879. Dollar. Same obverse and reverse excepting that this has " In God we Trust " above eagle and " One Dollar " is in smaller letters. 35.00.

1879. Dollar. Regular obverse ; rev., small eagle, ¾ face to right, with head turned to left, arrows and branch behind wings. Silver proof. 35.00.

1879. Dollar. Profile to left with wavy hair done up in a twist bound by a ribbon, inscribed "Liberty." Rev., similar eagle to last, but much smaller : two olive branches from below form a wreath extending near top of eagle's wings. Silver proof. 75.00.

1879. Silver metric and goloid dollars. Brilliant proofs. Pair for 4.00.

1880. Goloid Dollar. Barber's design. Silver proof. 20.00.

1882. Five Cents. Obverse and reverse same as regular issue without "Cents," excepting in date. Nickel proof. 3.50.

1882. Five Cents. "United States of America" around head. Reverse, V in corn and oak wreath, "E Pluribus Unum" above. Nickel proof. 3.50.

1882. Same as the regular issue of this year (old design), except that the shield on reverse is large and has no boll at bottom. Extremely rare. Nickel proof. 5.00.

1883. Five Cents. Same as the regular issue, excepting a band inscribed "Cents" on reverse over V. Nickel proof. 3.50.

1883. Five Cents. Same as regular issue without "Cents," but has word "Liberty" above head on obverse. Nickel proof. 3.50.

1883. Five Cents. Obverse, Liberty head surrounded by "United States of America." Reverses have a wreath of corn, cotton and sugar surrounded by 13 stars, 6 to right, 7 to left, "Five" above, "Cents" below. In the center is the percentage of metal: "50 N. 50 C.," "33 N. 67 C.," and "Pure Nickel." Nickel proofs. Set of 3 pieces. 25.00.

Foreign Crowns and Multiples of Crowns.

(All of crown size unless otherwise stated.)

Austria. 1549. Ferdinand I. Fine. 3.50.

1558. Ferdinand I. With title as Duke of Burgundy. Fine. 3.50.

1621. Leopold. Uncirculated. Brilliant mint lustre. 3.50.

1640. Ferdinand III. *Double Crown.* Uncirculated. 7.50.

1695. Leopold the Hogmouth. Broad Crown. Extremely fine. 2.50.

Brunswick. 1597. Henry Julius. "Truth" Crown. Scene of crucifixion, "Veritas" above. Fine. 3.00.

1599. Henry Julius. "Wasp" Crown. Lion and wasps. Very fine. 7.50.

1643. Augustus. "Bell" Crown. "Ao. 1643." Fine. 3.00.

1662. Christian. "Horse" Crown. Fine. 3.50.

1685. Rudolph Augustus. *Broad Triple Crown.* Female playing the lute, standing on a snail, mining scene and landscape in distance. Uncirculated. 30.00.

Brabant. 1567. Extremely fine. 3.50.

1622. Philip IV. Fine. 2.50.

1658. Philip IV. Very fine. 2.50.

Campen. 1597. Date between turrets of castle. Very good. 2.50.

Denmark. 1659. Frederick III. Sword dividing hand, date Feb. 2nd. Fine. Very rare. 4.00.

Genoa. 1631. Conrad II. (King of the Romans). Broad 1½ Crown. Very fine. Rare. 5.00.

1665. Thick Double Crown. Fine. 4.00.

Hamburg. 1600–1700. Marriage Triple Crown. Man and woman, hands joined. Extremely fine. 10.00.

1600–1700. Broad Baptismal Double Crown. Scene of Baptism in Jordan. Extremely fine. 5.00.

Mantua. Charles I. Rev., Sun progressing through signs of Zodiac, stars in field, world below. Extremely fine. Rare. 5.00.

Parma. 1627. Odoardo Farnese. Rev., bust of St. Antonius as a Roman soldier. Extremely fine. 3.00.

1631. Odoardo Farnese. Rev., St. Antonius carrying standard. Uncirculated. 3.50.

Fractional Currency.

(All new and clean.)

50, 25, 10, 5 Cents. Perforated edges. 5.00.
50, 25, 10, 5 Cents. Plain edges. 2.00.
50, 25, 10, 5 Cents. Washington in gilt ring. 2.50.
50, 25, 10, 5 Cents. Washington in gilt ring. Paper that will split. 5.00.
50 Cents. Justice. Red back. Auto. sign. of Colby and Spinner. Coarse fibre paper. 5.00.
50 Cents. Justice. Red back. Auto. sign. of Colby and Spinner. Plain paper. 3.50.
50 Cents. Justice. Red back. No letters on rev. 2.50.
50 Cents. Justice. Green back. Coarse fibre paper. 3.50.
50 Cents. Justice. Green back. 2.00.
50 Cents. Spinner. Red back. Auto. sign. of Allison and Spinner. 7.50.
50 Cents. Spinner. Red back. Auto. sign. of Colby and Spinner. 3.50.
50 Cents. Spinner. Red back. 2.25.
50 Cents. Spinner. Green back. "50" at ends. 1.50.
50 Cents. Spinner. Green back. "50" in centre. 1.75.
25 Cents. Fessenden. Red back. 1.50. Green back. .50.
25 Cents. Fessenden. Green back. Coarse fiber paper, gilt letters on reverse. Heavy but not solid disc. 5.00.
25 Cents. Fessenden. Green back. Coarse fiber paper. Solid discs. 20.00.
15 Cents. Grant and Sherman. Red back. Auto. sign. of Allison and Spinner. 8.00
15 Cents. Grant and Sherman. Red back. Auto. sign. of Jeffries and Spinner. Pasted together and used. 2.50.
10 Cents. Washington. Red back. Auto. sign. of Colby and Spinner. 1.50.
10 Cents. Washington. Red back. 1.00. Green back. .35.
5 Cents. Clark. Red back. .75. Green back. .35.
3 Cents. Washington. .40. Dark curtain. .75.
50 Cents. Lincoln. 1.50.
50 Cents. Stanton. .85.
25 Cents. Washington. .50. Same, blue at ends. .65.
15 Cents. Liberty. .60. Same, blue at ends. .75.
10 Cents. Liberty. .35. Same, blue at ends. .50.
1776. Quarter Dollar. Very fine. 2.00.
1777. Oct. 16. 20sh. Long note. Hand holding Constitution. Uncirculated. 5.00.
1778. $30. Blue hog. Very fine. 5.00.
Badges. Henry Clay. Portrait. Indian with shield above. .50.

Continental and Colonial Notes, Badges, Etc.

Continental. A nice Collection embracing the following notes: May 10, 1775.
$8. Nov. 29, 1775. $6. Feb. 17, 1776. $⅙, ⅓, ½, ⅔, 2, 4. May 9,
1776. $1, 7. July 22, 1776. $7, 30. Nov. 2, 1776. $2, 3, 4, 5, 6, 7.
Feb 26, 1777. $8. May 20, 1777. $6. Sept. 26, 1778. $5, 8, 40, 50,
60. Jan. 14, 1779. $2, 20, 30, 35, 40, 45, 50, 60, 65, 80. Mostly in
choicest condition, some 15 being uncirculated and with but few exceptions
balance in fine or very fine condition. 35 notes. 12.50.

1778. April 11. $4. Yorktown. Very fine. 5.00.
1778. April 11. $5. Yorktown. Fine. 5.00.

The following have " Payment secured by United States " and bear devices similar to the 1779 issue of Continental money. They can fairly be called the 1780 issue
and added to Continental series.

New Hampshire. 1780. $1, 2, 3, 4. 5, 7, 8, 20. Very fine. Cancelled. 3.00.
Massachusetts. 1780. $1, 2, 3, 4, 5, 7, 8. Very fine. Cancelled. Lot 2.00.
Rhode Island. 1780. $2. 3, 4, 5, 7, 8, 20. Very fine. 5.00.
New Hampshire. 1737. 2, 3, 5, 10 sh 1756. 10, 15, 30, 60 sh. Beaver,
deer, dog and swans. Rare reprints on 2 sheets from original plates. 2.50.
Vermont. 1781. Feb., 2s. 6d. Fine and excessively rare. 35.00.
Massachusetts. 1776. 2d. Codfish and Pine Tree. Fine. 2.50.
1776. 9d. Codfish and Pine Tree. Fine. 2.50.
1776. 4 sh. Codfish and Pine Tree. Fine. 2.50.
1778. 4d. Codfish and Pine Tree. Fine. 2.50.
1778. 6 pence. Codfish and Pine Tree. Very fine. 3 00.
1778. 4 sh. 6d. Codfish and Pine Tree. Very good. 2.00.
1779. 2 sh. 6d. Sun rising and Pine Tree. Fine but cancelled. 1.50.
1779. 5 sh. 4d. Sun rising and Pine Tree. Fine. 2.50.
1779. June 1. £15. Pine tree surrounded by rattlesnake. On end, " Massachusetts State Lottery, Class the Third." 6x9 inches. Beautiful condition.
2.00.
1780. Feb. 5. £15. Similar to last, equally choice. " Class the Fourth." 2.00.
1780. Jan. 1. £111. 1. 8. A remarkable note, 5x10 inches. Payable Mar. 1,
1783: " Both Principal and Interest to be paid in the then current money
of the State in a greater or less sum according as Five Bushels of Corn,
Sixty-Eight Pounds and four-sevenths of a Pound of Beef, Ten Pounds of
Sheeps Wool, and Sixteen Pounds of Sole Leather, are worth more or less
than One Hundred and Thirty Pounds current money." Very choice condition. 5.00.
1785. April 1. £100. Large square note, 7½ inches. Beautiful condition. 1.50.
1777. Jan. 22. £10 Large square note. 6½x8 inches. This note and the next
have a heavenly choir at top, 20 little angels with wings growing out of
their heads ornamenting the top. Fine. 2.00.
1777. Jan. 16. £10. Similar to last, but " Committee of War " at top. Beautiful
condition. 3.00.
Connecticut. 1775. June 1. 40 sh. This and some of the following have on
reverse four warty nosed angels with wings growing out of their heads,
tombstone style. Uncirculated. 1 50.
1776. June 7. 1, 2, 3 sh. First two uncirculated, clean cut cancellation; last
good. 2.50.
1776. June 19. 6, 9d., 2, 5 sh. First three uncirculated, scarcely perceptible
slight clean cut cancellation, last good. 3.00.
1777. Oct. 11. 2, 3, 4, 5, 7d. Small blue notes. Uncirculated, rare. 5.00.
1780. July 1. 2sh. 6d., 5, 40 sh. First uncirculated, 5 sh. good, 40 sh. very fine.
Clean cancellation. 2.00.

1658. **Philip IV.** Very fine. 2.50.
Campen. 1597. Date between turrets of castle. Very good. 2.50.
Denmark. 1659. Frederick III. Sword dividing hand, date Feb.
2nd. Fine. Very rare. 4.00.

1776. Aug. 13. $1/3. Fire. $3. Decalogue. $5. Candelabra. $10. Elephant. Good to fine. 5.00.

New Jersey. 1776. 3, 6, 15, 30 sh. Uncirculated. 1.00.

1781. 3 sh. 6d. Uncirculated. Rare. 1.50.

Pennsylvania. 1764. June 8. 20 sh. Printed by *Ben. Franklin.* Good. 1.00.

1769. 2 sh. 1771. 5, 10, 15 sh. 1772. 9d., 2 sh. 6d. 1775, April 10. 50 sh., Prison note. 1775, July 20. 40 sh. 1775. Oct. 25. 1. 2, 5 sh. 1776, April 25. 4, 6, 9d., 1, 1½, 2, 2½, 20 sh. 1777. 4. 9d. Long notes: red, 1 sh.; black, 1½, 2, 3, 4, 6, 12 sh. 1781. 9d, nearly uncir'd, rare. A very desirable collection in fair to uncir'd condition, average very good or fine. 29 notes. 5.00.

Delaware. 1758. May. 1. 20sh. Printed by Ben Franklin. Good. 1 00.

1759. June 1. 15, 20sh. Lion on reverse. Printed by Ben. Franklin. Weak at fold. 1.50.

1760. May 31. 40 sh. Printed by Ben. Franklin. Good but mended. .75.

1776. 4, 5, 10, 20 sh. 1777. 2½ sh. Good to uncir'd. 1 00.

Maryland. 1774. $1/3, 8. 1775. $1/3, 2. 1776. $1/6, 1/3, ½, 4. Good to uncirculated. 8 notes. 1.50.

Virginia. 1775. Arms of Virginia. 1 sh. 3d., 2 sh. 6d., 5 sh. Fine and rare. 4.00.

1776. "Sic Semper Tyrannis." $6, 8, 10, 15. 1778. $10. Very fine. 3.00.

1780. July. $13⅓, 45, 55, 60, 80, 100. 1780, Oct. $50, 100, 200, 300, 400, 500. 1781, March. $250, 500, 1000. Tissue paper notes. A few a little ragged, as usual, but an exceptionally nice lot, with nearly all the values, including the highest. The rare notes, including the $13⅓ and $1000, are very fine.

North Carolina. 1768. 20 sh. Fine. 1.00.

1771. 2 sh. 6d. House. 5 sh. Inkstand. £1. Leopard. Very good and fine. 3.00.

1775. Aug. 21. $5. Group of buildings. Good but has been folded. 1.00.

1776, April 2. $2½. Hand holding arrows. $5. Bird. $6. Goat. $6. Squirrel. $7½. British flag. $8. Cock (a little torn). $8. Leopard. Fine and rare lot. 7 notes. 10.00.

1778. $¼. "Independence." $5. "Behold, a new world." $10. "Persecution the ruin of empires." $20. "American Virtue triumphant." $25, 50. Very fine. 4.00.

1780. $25 (2). Different mottoes. Very fine. 1.25.

South Carolina. 1775, June 1. £10. Sword in hand. Very large note. Good. 1 00.

1775, Nov. 13. £2. 10 sh. Crossed swords. "Pro Libertate." Very fine and rare. 5.00.

1776, March 6. £15. Lion. Fine. 1.00.

1776, Oct. $2. Bush. $4. Elephant. $6, 8. Storm on land and sea. $2, a little torn, $4 good, $6 and $8 very fine. Rare lot. 10.00.

1776, Dec. 23. $2, 3, 4. Uncirculated sheet of 6 notes, two of each. 2.00.

1776, Dec 23. $1. Tree on rock. $3. Fortification. $4. Ship on fire. $8. Ship. $20. Cow. Lot, 1.50.

1777. $20. Bird flying from cage. Very fine. 1.00.

1778, Apr. 10. 2sh. 6d., cornucopiæ. 3sh. 9d., beaver. 5sh., phœnix. 10sh., palmetto tree. Uncirculated, one sheet. 1.50.

1778. 7 sh. 6d. Bee-hive. 20 sh. Horse. Fine and rare. 2.00.

1779. $40. Fame blowing trumpet, Continental flags. $50. Hercules carrying large stone. $60. Lyre, trumpets and flags. $70. Prometheus chained to a rock, a vulture preying on his vitals. $80. Musical implements. $90. Hercules strangling a lion. Large notes. Very fine and uncirculated. 7.50.

Georgia. 1776. 2 sh. 6d. Horse. Large note. Very fine. 7.50.

1776. Quarter Dollar. Very fine. 2.00.

1777. Oct. 16. 20sh. Long note. Hand holding Constitution. Uncirculated. 5.00.

1778. $30. Blue hog. Very fine. 5.00.

Badges. Henry Clay. Portrait. Indian with shield above. .50.

Lafayette. Old, 1824 probably. 1.00.
Washington. Centennial Celebration, 1832. .50.
American Manufactures and Ireland's Independence Solidarity with attached medal, size 24, " We purpose 'fore high heaven till Erin's chains are riven," etc. .50.
Broken Bank Bills. A great variety, from poor to uncirculated. *All different.* 75 notes. Lot, 10.00.
Broken Bank Bills. Good to uncirculated. All different. 17 pcs. 1.50.
Hungarian Fund. $1. Louis Kossuth. 1852. Fine. 1.00.
Card Checks. War necessity money. 5, 25, 75 cts., J. M. Christy. .75.
$1000. Mechanics Bank of Augusta, Ga. 1856. Slightly mended but fine. I have never seen so high a value in Bank Bills. 2.50.
Cuba. 1869. ½ and 1 Peso. Uncirculated. Pair, .50.
Republic of Ireland. $10. Large note. Signed by Michael Scanlan. 2.50.
Andrew Johnson. Impeachment Tickets. 4 colors. 150. Lot, 2.50.

Confederate Notes.

1861. $100. Montgomery. Train of cars to right. Fine. 10.00.
1861. $100. Richmond. Train of cars to left. Uncirculated. 15.00.
1861. $50. Montgomery Negroes hoeing cotton. Uncirculated. 7.50.
1861. Sept. 2. $5. Group of females. Letters A, B and C. 3 pcs. Very good. Lot 5.00.
1861. Sept. 2. $5. Group of females. Letter A. Very good. 2.00.
1864. Set from 50 cts. to $500. 1.00.

The following lot of Confederate notes were collected by the late Geo. Mason, for many years a dealer in stamps, paper money, etc. The lots contain some duplicates, but the former owner collected all the varieties he could secure, and collectors of varieties will find the following a rich field to glean from.

$5, $10, $20, $50, $100. Richmond, Sept. 2, 1861. Good to uncirculated. 152 notes. 25.00.
$1, $2, $5, $10, $20. Issue of Dec. 2, 1862. 1st and 2d series. Good to uncirculated. 123 notes. 12.50.
$100 Interest notes, 1862-63. (II. 55.) Long and short, thick and thin paper, different watermarks, lettering, etc. Includes 10 of the rare note with "The" wanting before "Confederate." Good to uncirculated. 273 notes. 45.00.
$100 Interest notes. (II. 56, 57, 58, 59, 60) Long and short letters, different watermarks, etc. Includes several varieties not in II. Largely uncirculated 382 notes. 60.00.
.50, $1, $2, $5, $10, $20, $50, $100. Issues of 1863. A fine selection, embracing almost all varieties. General condition very good, many uncirculated. 296 notes. 30.00.
.50, $1, $2, $5, $10, $20, $50, $100, $500. Issues of 1864. Embraces almost all varieties and many scarce specimens. All but a few pieces uncirculated. 958 notes. 100.00.

The following C. S. A. notes are cancelled with clean x x cuts, nothing missing from note, and could be easily mended so as to make cancellation imperceptible.

1861. Sept. 2. $50. Train of cars. Very fine. 2.00.
1861. Sept. 2. $20. Female and globe. Very fine. 1.50.
1861. Sept. 2. $10. Group of Indians. Fine. 1.50.
1861. Sept. 2. $10. Wagon loaded with cotton bales. Very fine. Scarce. 2.00.
1861. Sept. 2. $5. Group of females. Practically uncirculated. 2.00.
Confederate Note Album. Bechtel's. With 42 notes, nearly all uncirculated, and some very scarce, mounted in proper spaces in the album. 8.50.
C. S. A. $100 Bond. Act of Feb. 28, 1861. Haseltine No. 5. A little stained. .75.
C. S. A. $100. Bond. Feb. 17, 1864. Fine. .75.
Mixed lot of C. S. A. (including a lot of poor $1 and $2 bills) and Southern State notes. Great variety. Poor to good. 1024 notes. 10.00.

Foreign Crowns and Multiples of Crowns.

(All of Crown or Dollar size unless otherwise stated.)

Austria. 1569. Maximilian II. Fine. 3 00.
1572. Ferdinand. Very fine. 3.00.
1603. Rudolph II. Very fine. 2.50.
1612. Rudolph II. Very fine. 2 50.
1630. Ferdinand II. Very good. 1.75.
—— Ferdinand II. Crown without date. Fine. 1.50.
1632. Leopold. Very fine. 2.25.
1639. Ferdinand IV. Fine. 2.00.
——. Leopold and Claudia. Double Crown. Fine. 5.00.
1661. Leopold. Very good. 1.75.
Brunswick. 1638. Frederick. Gothic designs. Very good. 2.00.
—— Augustus. Ship's Crown. Very fine. 5.00.
1658. George William. "Wild man" crown. Uncirculated. 4.00.
1664. Christian Louis. Broad mining Double Crown. Horse crowned by hand issuing from cloud over mine; rev., crowned monogram surrounded by 14 crowned shields. Very fine; rare. Size 40. 25.00.
Burgundy. 1618. Maximilian. Very fine. 2.50.
Denmark. 1652. Frederick. Crown of 4 Marks. Crowned profile; rev., a crown. Very fine. 3.50.
1659. Frederick. Crown on the repulse of the Swedes; royal cypher on a rock which divides EBEN EZER; rev., a hand from a cloud cuts off with a sabre another hand which reaches towards a crown. Rare and fine. 4.00.
Frankfurt. 1776. Crown. Francofurtia with shield and river gods. Fine. 1.75.
Guelders. 1568. Philip II. of Spain. Very good. 2.50.
1616. Good. 1.25.
Genoa. 1633. Conrad II. Triple Crown. Griffons supporting crowned cypher; rev., short cross, cherub heads in angles. Fine and rare. Size 37. 15.00.
1685. 1½ Crown. Virgin and Infant. Very good. 3.50.
Holland. 1672. Triple Crown. Knight on horseback. Very fine. 10.00.
Hesse-Darmstadt. Ernest Louis. Crown. 1697. Shield of-arms hanging to palm tree, male figure at each side; rev., mining scene at sunrise. Very fine and extremely rare, edge lettered. 6 00.
Kaufbeuren. Charles V. Crown. 1545. Crowned profile in armor; rev., shield, MONE : NOVI : CIVITATIS : KAVFBVREN. Fine; very rare. 5.00.
Leuchtenberg. George, Landgrave. Crown. 1547. Knight holds shield and banneret. Sharp, uncirculated, rare. 5.00.
Papal States. Urban VIII. (1623–1644.) Scudo, year XI. Bust r.; rev., St. Michael and the dragon, VIVET DEVS. Fine. 3.50.
(1670–1676.) Clement X. Jubilee Scudo, 1675. Altiera arms; rev., pilgrims advancing toward the *Porta Santa* in St. Peter's. Sharp, uncirculated, rare. 3.50.
(1676–1689.) Innocent XI. Scudo, year 2. Bust; rev., facade of St. Peter's, PORTAE INFERI NON PRAEVALEBUNT. Very fine. 3.50.
(1681–1790.) Innocent XII. Scudo. 1698. Rev., St. Peter giving his benediction. Very fine. 3.50.
Piacenza. Alexander Farnese. Crown. 1590. Portrait bust of this great general and enemy of Elizabeth of England; rev., female between the river-god Po and she-wolf guarding the arms of Piacenza, PLAC. ROMAN. COLON. Very fine. Extremely rare. 12.50.
Palatinate. Frederick II., Elector. Crown. 1547. Bust facing, in imperial crown and robes, holds sword and globe; rev., three shields surmounted by crowned lion on crests. Extremely fine, very rare. 5.00.
Ratzburg. Frederic. Crown. 1640. Bust in bishop's robe. Fine and rare. 4.00.
Stolberg. Wolfgang George. Broad Crown. 1624. Stag. Very fine. Rare. 6.00.
Salzburg. Wolfgang, Theodore. No date. Very good. 1.25.

1619.   St. Rupert seated ; rev , ram. Fine   2.00.
1624.   St. Rupert; rev., virgin and child. Fine. 1.75.
1628.   Two bishops holding up cathedral ; rev., procession of priests carrying relig-
ious emblems. Very fine. 3.00.
1708.   John Ernest. Uncirculated. Brilliant mintlustre. 2.50.
St. Gall   1624. " Bear Crown." Fine. 3.00.
Schaffhausen. 1621. Ram springing from temple door. Very good. 2.50.
Schwarzenberg. 1696. Ferdinand and Maria Anna. Busts jugata. Very fine. 2.50.
Saxony. 1535. John Fred. and George. Fine. 3.00.
1540.   John Fred.; rev., bust of Henry. Very fine. 3.50.
1583.   John and Fred. Wm. Bust on each side. Good. 2.50.
1593.   " Three Dukes " Crown. Fine. 2.25.
1598.   " Three Dukes " Crown. Very fine. 3.00.
1606.   Christian II. with drawn sword ; rev., busts of John George and Augustus
facing. Very fine. 2.50.
1620.   " Four -Dukes " Crown. Three busts in procession ; rev., bust. Uncirculated. 3.50.
1623.   Full figure of Saxonia; rev., large crested shield. Sharp, brilliant, uncirculated and rare. 5.00.
1624.   Busts of Wm., Fred. and Fred. Ernest. Barely circulated. 3.50.
1625   John George. Bust with drawn sword. Barely circulated. 3.50.
1630.   John George. Half crown, Crown and Double Crown. Centennial of Augs-
burg Confession. An almost uncirculated set. 12.50.
1635.   John George. Fine. 2.50
1652.   John George. Uncirculated. Mint lustre. 3.50.
1657.   John George II. The duke on horseback ; rev., name and titles in 12 lines.
Sharp, brilliant, uncirculated. 5.00.
1661.   John George II. Broad Double Crown (over 2½ in. in diameter). Monu-
ment. To left; open book, crowned, with snake on cross and Christ on
cross—to right; crossed swords and cap. Extremely fine. 10.00.
1680.   John George II. Broad Mortuary Crown. Father Time prostrate under a
trophy of shields, from which triumphant Fame arises ; rev., inscription in
16 lines. Sharp, uncirculated. Very rare. Size 31. 7.50.
Saxe-Weimar. 1619. John Ernest. Bust of the duke, around which are grouped
the busts of his seven children. Fine. Rate. 5.00.
Spain. 1561. Philip II. Very good. 3.50.
1563.   Philip II. Half Crown. Very good. 1.25.
1684.   Charles II. Crown. Bust ; reverse, crowned sceptre between two globes.
First coin representing America. California is depicted as an island.
Fine. 3.50.
Tuscany. 1679. Cosmus III. Crown. Bust in armor ; rev., baptism of Christ
by St. John. Extremely fine. 3.50.
1685.   Cosmus III. Crown. Rev., Port of Leghorn with lighthouse, ships, etc.
Fine. 3.00.
1711.   Cosmus III. Crown. Draped bust ; rev., crowned gate, whence the name,
" Tallere de la Torre." Very fine. 3.00.
Venice. John Cornaro I. (1625–1630.) Lion of St. Mark on shield. Very
good. 2.50.
Wittenberg. 1661. Reformation Crown. Bust of Luther; rev., view of the city.
Nearly uncirculated. Rare. 4.00.
West Frisia. 1596. *Double Crown.* Neptune on sea monster. Very good. 6.00.
1597.   Bust with sword. Good. 2.50.
1601.   Lions. *Double Crown.* Uncirculated. 10.00.
Wurzburg. 1693. John Godfried. Full figure of St. Kilianus with sword and
crook. Beautiful impression, extremely fine. 4.00.

Silver Siege and Necessity Coins.

Breda. 1625. Diamond shape. Size 14. Very fine. 2.50.
Carthagena. 1873. 2 and 5 Pesetas. Struck while the Centralists besieged the
city. Uncirculated. Very rare. Pair for 6.00.

Campen. 1578. Siege Crown of 42 Stubers. Arms of the city, CAMPEN, 42
    ST., 1578. Diamond shape. Fine and rare. 7.50.
Gotha. 1567. Siege crown. Very fine. 3.50.
Haarlem. 1572. Oblong. Size 16x20. Fine. Very rare. 4.00.
Majorca. 1821. Ferd. VII. Siege Dollar. Uncirculated. 3.00.
Middleburg. 1572. Square Siege Crown. Extremely fine. 5.00.
Munster. 1660. Square Siege Crown. Extremely fine. 5.00.
Minden. 1624. Oblong Siege Coin for 8 Groschen. Very fine. 2.00.
Saragossa. 1809. Ferd. VII. Siege Dollar. Uncirculated. 3.00.

Jewish Coins.

Judas Aristobulus. B. C. 106. *Widow's Mite.* Good. Very rare. Reigned only
    1 year. 3.50.
Alexander Januus. B. C. 105. *Widow's Mite.* Fine but slightly misstruck. 2.00.
Procurator under Augustus. A. D. 6–14. *Widow's Mite.* Very good. 2.50.
Gratus. Procurator under Tiberius. A. D. 14–25. *Widow's Mite.* Good. 2.00.
Herod Agrippa I. A. D. 37. (The Herod the King of Acts xii. 1.) *Mite.*
    Wheat heads and royal umbrella. Very good. 2.00.
Claudius Felix, Procurator under Nero. *Mite.* Two palm branches crossed. Good.
    2.00.
Claudius Felix. *Mite.* Two shields crossed; rev., palm tree. Good. 2.00.
Claudius Felix. *Mite.* Palm branch. Fine. 2.00.
First Revolt of the Jews. A. D. 66. Two handled vase; rev., grape leaf. Good.
    2.00.
Same but vase with cover. Good. 2.00.
Vespasian. A. D. 70. Denarius. Rev., captive beside armor, "Judæa" below.
    Struck to commemorate the destruction of Jerusalem. Fine. 3.00.
Vespasian. A. D. 70. Great bronze. Rev., captive under tree, soldier watching,
    "Judæa Capta." Very good. 7.50.

Roman Bronze, etc.

As. Early type. 500 B. C. Double head of Janus; rev., prow of vessel. Weight
    9 oz. Fine. 7.50.
Quadrans. Early type. Boar on each side. Fine. 2.50.
Sextans. Early type. Head of Minerva; rev., prow. Fine. 2.50.
Aes. Reduced type. Double head of Janus; rev., prow. Fine. 1.50.
Semis. Reduced type. Head of Jupiter; rev., prow. Very fine. 1.00.
Egypt. Large Bronze. Head of Jupiter; rev., eagle. Fine. Size 28. Weight
    3¼ oz. 2.50.
Egypt. Similar. Size 25. Fine. Weight 1¾ oz. 1.50.
Caliphs of Bagdad. Heads and squatting figures. Good to fine, one pierced. 7
    pcs. 2.50.
Herculaneum. Lead coins from ruins. As usually found. 8 pcs. 2.00.
Augustus and Agrippa. Rev., crocodile chained to palm tree. COL. NEM. (Colony
    Nemausus). Fine. 1.50.

Roman Silver Denarii.

Pompey the Great. Born 106 B. C. Head between lituus and vase. Very good.
    3.50.
M. Junius Brutus. Head, "Libertas." Rev., procession of lictors, BRUTUS below.
    Very fine. 2.50.
Julius Cæsar. "Imper Cæsar." Portrait. Rev., Venus Nicephore standing hold-
    ing a victory and hasta. Moneyer's name, "M. Mettius." Very fine. 4.00.
Julius Cæsar. Head of Venus to right; rev., two Gaulish captives under a trophy,
    "Cæsar" below. Good. 1.50.
Julius Cæsar. Portrait. "Dict. Perpetuo Cæsar." Rev., Venus seated. Very
    good. 3.00.
Julius Cæsar. Venus; rev., Aeneas carrying Anchiles. Fine. 2.50.

Augustus Cæsar. B. C. 31. Youthful head. "C. Cæsar III." Uncirculated. 3.00.
Galba. A. D. 68. Good. 1.00.
Otho. A. D. 69. Fine and rare. 3.00.
Vitellius. A. D. 69. Fine and rare. 3.00.
Vespasian. A. D. 70. Extremely fine. 1.50.
Titus. A. D. 79. Very good. Scarce. 1.50.
Domitian. A. D. 81. Fine. 1.00.
Nerva. A. D. 96. Very good. 1.00.
Trajan. A. D. 98. Extremely fine. 1.50.
Hadrian. A. D. 117. *Double Denarius.* Very good. Rare. 2.00.
Hadrian. A. D. 117. Rev., star and crescent. Very good. 1.00.
Antonius Pius. A. D. 138. Very fine. 1.00.
Septimus Severus. A. D. 193. Barely circulated. 1.00.
Geta. * A. D. 211. Fine. .75.
Elagabalus. A. D. 218. About uncirculated. 1.00.
Severus Alexander. A. D. 222. Extremely fine. 1.00.
Philip the Arab. A. D. 244. Extremely fine. .75.

Ancient Greek Coins.

Tetradrachms. Athens. Archaic style. 525 B. C. Head of Athena ; rev., owl Very fine. 5.00.
Macedonia. Alexander the Great. 336 B. C. *As it dropped from the die.* The sharpest and handsomest specimen I have seen. 15.00.
Syracuse. 400 B. C. Head of Arethusa surrounded by dolphins. Rev., Victory in biga. Very good. 4.00.
Thrace. B. C. 323. Lysimachus. Head of the deified Alexander with Ammon horn. Rev., Pallas Nikephoras seated. Fine. 5.00.
Didrachms. Aegina. Earliest period. 700 B. C. Turtle ; rev., punch marks. Fine. 5.00.
Agrigentum. 472 B. C. Sea eagle and crab. Fine. 2.00.
Chios. 500 B. C. Seated griffin ; rev., punch marks. Fine. 4.00.
Caulonia. 480 B. C. Nude slinger and stag; rev., stag. Fine. 2.50.
Crotona. 550 B. C. Tripod, stork; rev., incused. Fine. 3.50.
Gela. 466 B. C. Man-headed bull : rev., horseman. Fine. 3.50.
Metapontum 500 B. C. Ear of wheat ; the same incused. Very fine. 3.50.
Posidonia. Neptune ; rev., bull. Very good. 1.50.
Sybaris. 550 B. C. Broad Didrachm. Bull with head turned back ; rev., same incused. Fine. 7.50.
Tarentum. 360 B. C. Naked horseman ; rev., Taras on dolphin. Fine. 2.00.
Thasos. 465 B. C. Satyr on knee bearing a nymph in his arms ; rev., punch mark. Fine. 5.00.
Velia. 400 B. C. Head of Pallas ; rev., lion devouring a skull. Fine. 2.50.
Egypt. Ptolemy VIII. 146 B. C. Didrachm. Head ; rev., eagle. Fine. 2.00.
Drachms. Cnidus. Thick. Head of Venus in sunken square ; rev., lion's head. Fine. 2.00.
Dyrrhachium. Cow suckling calf. Very fine. 2.00.
Spain. Head; rev., horseman. Very good. 1.00.
Sybaris. 530 B. C. Bull ; rev., incused. Very good. 2.50.
Hemi-Drachms. Cherosonesus. Forepart of lion. Fine. .75.
Caria. Lion's head and star. Very fine. 1.00.
Histiæa. Bacchante head ; rev., female on prow. Extremely fine. 1.00.
Macedonia. Philip II. Head ; rev., horseman. Very good. 1.00.
Messana. Hare. Fine. 1.00.
Miletas. Head; rev., lion. Fine. .50.
Rhodes. An early type. Head ; rev., flower in incused square. Very good. 1.00.
Sinope. Head ; rev., harpy eagle. Good. .50.

Sicyon. Lion and dove. Good. .50.
Thurium. Head; rev., bull. Very good. .75.
Persia. Darius I. 521 B. C. King as an archer. Rev., punch mark. Silver Daric. Very good. Rare. 5.00.
Parthia. Drachms. Obverse, head of king; reverse, king seated. No duplicates. Very good to very fine. Nice lot. 14 pcs. Lot 7.00.

Peace Medals.

Libertas Americana. 1783. Louis XVI. on throne pointing to an American shield which a female is hanging on a pillar surmounted by a liberty cap; rev., Minerva holding shield. Tin. Very good. Size 29. Rare. 1.50.
Louis XVIII; rev., pedestal, America and France on either side; "Gallia et America fœderata, etc." Bronze proof. Size 32. 1.50.
1781. Netherlands. Four shields linked, "Gewapende Neutraliteit;" rev., "Jehovah," etc., in ten lines. Silver. Dull proof. 2.50.
Figure of Netherlands standing; "Netherland declares America free." Rev., a staff bearing flags of Holland and U. S., bales of goods and ship. "The Universal Wish, 1782." Silver proof. Size 22. 5.00.

Washington Medals.

Bust to left; George Washington, by F. B. Smith & Hartmann, N. Y.; rev., tomb of Washington; above, Fame flying. Bronze proof. Rare. Size 41. 5.00.
Bust to right, Paquet; rev., cabinet of Washington medals in U. S. Mint. Bronze. proof. Size 38. 1.25.
Rare silver temperance token by Bale, size 12, pierced. 1.00.
Westwood medal. Bust to right; rev., "Made commander-in-chief," etc. Bronze. Size 26. 5.00.
Head to left. George Washington. Rev., "Born Feb. 22d, 1732," etc., in 6 lines Silver proof. Weight 2 oz. Size 29. 3.00.
Liberty crowning bust of Washington on pedestal. Rev., Benevolence helping fallen man. 1808. Washington Benevolent Society, New York. Silver. Dull proof. Size 27. 2.00.
Washington. Rev., sword and fasces on altar. The Halliday medal. Very fine. Size 34. 2.50.
Bust; reverses, the different battles of 1776. Set of 8 pieces. Copper proofs. Size 22. 3.00.

Presidential Medals.

James Madison. Bust to right; rev., eagle, scroll, etc., w. m. proof. Size 40. 1.00.
James Monroe. Peace Medal. Bronze proof. Size 48. 1.50.
John Quincy Adams. Peace Medal. Br. proof. Size 48. 1.50.
Andrew Jackson. Peace Medal. Br. proof. Size 48. 1.50.
Same. Copper proof. Size 40. 1.00.
Zachary Taylor. For Palo Alto. Bronze proof. Size 40. 1.50.
View of the Battle of Buena Vista; rev., pelican feeding young. Presented to Gen. Taylor by Louisiana. Bronze proof. Size 48. 3.00.
Zachary Taylor. Peace Medal. Bronze proof. Size 48. 1.50.
Millard Fillmore. Bust to right, 1850; rev., Pioneer and Indian before an American flag. Bronze proof. Size 40. 1.50.
James Buchanan. "Embassy from Japan." Bronze proof. Size 48. 1.50.
Same. "To Frederick Rose, Ass't Surgeon U. S. Navy." Group of figures. Bronze proof, slightly stained on edge. Size 48. 1.50.
Abr. Lincoln. Rev., Indian plowing. scalping scene, etc. Bronze proof. Size 40. 2.00.
Andrew Johnson. Rev., draped female with American flag grasping the hand of an Indian before a bust of Washington on a pedestal. Silver proof. Size 48. Weighs 6⅛ oz. Av. 10.00.
U. S. Grant. Bust, "The oceans united by railway, May 10, 1869;" rev., mountain scenery, train of cars, etc. Silver proof. Size 28. 2.50.

Miscellaneous American Medals.

John Egar Howard. For battle of Cowpens. Bronze proof. Size 29. 1.00.
Wm. Washington, same battle, bronze proof, size 29. 1.00.
"Light horse Harry" Lee, for battle of Paulus Hook, N. J., 1779. Silver. Dull
    proof. Size 29. 3.50.
Col. Geo. Crogan. Defense of Fort Stephenson, 1813; rev., view of the battle.
    Bronze proof. Size 40. 1.50.
Gov. Isaac Shelby, for battle of Thames, 1813; rev , view of the battle. Bronze
    proof. Size 40. 1.50.
Maj.-Gen'l. Winfield Scott, for battle of Chippewa. Bronze proof. Size 40. 1.50.
Thos. Truxton; rev., scene of naval victory. Bronze proof. Size 36. 1.50.
Capt. James Biddle, capture of Penguin, 1815; rev., naval battle. Bronze proof.
    Size 40. 1.50.
Capt. Johnston Blakely, capture of Reindeer; rev., naval battle. Bronze proof. Size
    40. 1.50.
John Paul Jones. For victories off Scottish coast; rev., naval scene. Bronze proof.
    Size 36. 1.00.
Franklin; by Dupre; rev., "Eripuit Cœlo," etc., in wreath. Bronze proof. Size 29.
    1.25.
Franklin; rev., angel, br. proof, size 29. 1.25.
Franklin, bust in fur cap; rev., Franklin Institute, Pa. Bronze proof. Size 24. 1.00.
Lafayette, by Cannois; rev., "Appele pane volu unanime, etc." Silver. Dull proof.
    Size 32. Weight 2½ oz. Av. 5.00.
Lafayette, by Cannois; rev., "The defender," etc. Bronze proof. Size 30. 1.25.
Henry Clay; rev., hand on rock, inscribed "Constitution." Bronze proof. Size 48.
    3.00.
Wreck of Steamer Metis; rev., life-saving scene. Bronze proof. Size 40. 2.50.
Rescue of crew of U. S. Brig Somers, 1846; scene of wreck; rev., scene of rescue.
    Bronze proof. Size 36. 2.00.
Humane Society of Massachusetts, 1866; shield with ship and boats, surmounted by
    house of refuge. Bronze proof. Size 36. 2.00.
Tayleur medal, "Fund for shipwrecked strangers," view of shipwreck. Bronze
    proof. Size 28. Rare. 2.00.
Sanitary Fair, Philadelphia, 1864, sick soldier, etc. Bronze proof. Size 36. 1.50.
Dr. Elisha Kane, bust above Arctic scene; rev., Masonic emblems. Bronze proof.
    Size 32. 1.25.
Agassiz, bust to right. Bronze proof. Size 29. 1.25.
Washington Irving ; rev., date of birth. Bronze proof. Size 44. 3.50.
A. Thiers, from Philadelphia, 1873. Bronze proof. Size 29. 1.25.
Cyrus W. Field, for Atlantic Cable. Bronze proof. Size 32. 1.00.
Same. White metal proof. .25.
California State Agri. Soc. Award medal. Handsome landscape scene with ani-
    mals including a large bear, fruits, etc. Very fine. Size 28. Weight 1¼
    oz. Av. 2.00.
1849. Salem Charitable Mech. Assoc. Hercules has just killed a winged dragon ;
    boys picking apples from an impossible tree. Size 28. Bronze proof. 1.25.

Centennial Medals.

Centennial Commission Medal. Size 36. Bronze proof in velvet lined morocco
    case. .75. Brass proof. In case. .50. W. M. proof. In case. .50.
Same. Smaller, size 24. Silver proof. 1.25.
Same as last, brass proof in case. .40.
Independence Hall: legend, "Proclaim Liberty, etc.;" rev., Memorial Hall, "To
    commemorate," etc. Bronze proof, size 37, in case. The handsomest U.
    S. Centennial Medal. 2.00.
French Centennial. Beautiful head of Liberty; rev., crossed flags. Beautiful, ex-
    ceeds anything issued in U S. Bronze proof. Size 32. 2.50.
Brazilian Centennial. Dom Pedro II. (The king that has been lately overthrown).
    "Exposicao Internaceonal de Philadelphia, 1876." Very fine and rare. 1.50.

Halifax Ferry Token. Steamboat. Bright red proof. 2.00.
White's Farthing, Halifax. Very fine. 5.00.
Francis Mullins & Son. Very fine. 1.00.
Robert Purvis. Uncirculated. .75.
H. Gagnon. Beaver. Extremely fine. Olive. 1.00.
T. S. Brown & Co. Fine. Brown. .35.
Hostermann & Etter. 1815. Fine. .35.
Magdalen Island. Seal and dried codfish. Fine. 1.50.
Montreal and Lachine Railroad Co. Engine and beaver. Large. Extra fine.
    3.00.
Nova Scotia and New Brunswick. Ship, "Success" below. Very fine. 5.00.

Ancient and Foreign Gold.

Turkey. Gold. Proof. Size 14. 2.00.
Transylvania. 1657. George Rakoczi II. Ducat. Uncirculated. 6.00.
Salzburg. 1714. Francis Anton. ½ Ducat. Uncirculated. 2.00.
Nordlingen. 1497. Ducat. The 4 in loop form. One of the earliest dated coins.
Lord Bacon, bust nearly facing; rev., Learning with starry robe flying over world.
    Silver proof. 27. 4.00.
Napoleon, rev., copy of star of legion of honor. Beautiful. 26. 2.00.
Napoleon, bust in cocked hat; rev., urn and sword, etc., funeral medal, 1840, by
    Roget, very beautiful. 33. 2.50.
Napoleon; rev's., Fabius Cunctator, orphan of Legion of Honor, Egyptian eagle, the
    Alps, etc. Silver proof or nearly proof. Size 25. Weight about 1⅓ oz.
    Av. each. 7 pcs. Lot 20.00.
Louis Philippe; rev., France offering the crown, Aug. 9, 1830. Beautiful. 48.
    3.50.
Louis Philippe, busts of king and queen in separate medallions facing; rev., medal-
    lions with heads of the whole royal family surrounded with allegorical fig-
    ures. A magnificent medal, exquisitely designed. 50. 3.50.
Napoleon III. Rev., Empress. By Montagny. 34. 2.00.
.... p...... ...., ...e. 0.00.

Oriental Silver.

Madras. Quarter Pagoda. Tower surrounded by stars; rev., god Vishnu in circle
    of dots. Fine. 1.50.
Assam. Octagonal Rupee. Very fine. Rare. 2.00.
Burmah. Rupee and ⅛ Rupee. Peacock with spread tail. Very fine. 2.00.
Japan. Itzebue. Uncirculated. .75.
Japan. ¼ Itzebue. Uncirculated. .35.
Siam. Bullet money. Tical. Very fine. 1.25.
Siam. Bullet money. ¼ and ⅛ Tical. Very fine. Each .75.
Persia. ¼ Kran. Sun-lion with sword (dime size). Uncirculated. .50.
Japan. Oblong, one pear shaped, silver dumps, each stamped with characters.
    They range in size from a pea to ¾ oz. I do not think two sizes are alike.
    Fine lot. 13 pieces. 12.50.
Japan. Dragon and sun. Yen (Dollar), semi-proof; Sen, proof; 10 and 5 Sen,
    uncirculated. Lot 3.00.
Siam. Circulars coin with elephant and royal umbrellas. 2, 1, ⅛, ¹₁₆ Tical. About
    uncirculated. 5.00.
Cambodia. Bird idol. Very fine. Size 8. .50.
England. William IV. 1830. A superb frosted silver medal by Chantry, sur-
    rounded by projecting silver band to protect medal. Bust to right; rev.,
    "Adelaide regina cudi jussit, 1830," in wreath with trident. Extremely
    fine. Excessively rare. Weight 5 oz. Size 44. 12.50. .... 7.50.
China. Spanish Dollar covered with Chinese chop marks, a number of which are
    die-stamps of various designs. 2.50.
Cambodia. Tical. Odd looking bird. Rev., turreted temple. Uncirculated. 5.00.
Madras. Half and Quarter Pagoda. Tower surrounded by stars; rev., God Vishnu

Miscellaneous American Medals.

John Egar Howard. For battle of Cowpens. Bronze proof. Size 29. 1.00.
Wm. Washington, same battle, bronze proof, size 29. 1.00.
"Light horse Harry" Lee, for battle of Paulus Hook, N. J., 1779. Silver. Dull proof. Size 29. 3.50.
Col. Geo. Crogan. Defense of Fort Stephenson, 1813; rev., view of the battle. Bronze proof. Size 40. 1.50.
Gov. Isaac Shelby, for battle of Thames, 1813; rev, view of the battle. Bronze proof. Size 40. 1.50.
Maj.-Gen'l. Winfield Scott, for battle of Chippewa. Bronze proof. Size 40. 1.50.
Thos. Truxton; rev., scene of naval victory. Bronze proof. Size 36. 1.50.
Capt. James Biddle, capture of Penguin, 1815; rev., naval battle. Bronze proof. Size 40. 1.50.
Capt. Johnston Blakely, capture of Reindeer; rev., naval battle. Bronze proof. Size 40. 1.50.
John Paul Jones. For victories off Scottish coast; rev., naval scene. Bronze proof.

Masonic Medals.

Hopkins Lodge, Black Jack Grove, Texas. Silver, brass and copper proofs. Size 14. Lot 1.00.
Hermit Commandery, No. 24, Lebanon, Pa. Beautiful nine-pointed bronze medal (size 34) in the centre of which is handsome relief design of cave, knight greeting hermit. Mounted on the ribbon are also triangle (size 25) with name of commandery and small oval with "24." 5.00.
Triennial Conclave, San Francisco. Knight on horseback. Gold. Size 8. 1.00.
Egyptain Obelisk. Marvin 712. Silver proof. Size 22. 1.50.
Same. Bronze proof. .75
Philadelphia Commandery, No. 2. Bell-shaped Centennial. Silvered. Perfect. Size 32x32. 50.
Olive Branch, No. 39, N. Y. W. metal proof. Size 26. .25.
Huinahe Commandery, No. 23. Phila. W. metal, proof, size 29. .35.
house of refuge. Bronze proof. Size 36. 2.00.
Tayleur medal, "Fund for shipwrecked strangers," view of shipwreck. Bronze proof. Size 28. Rare. 2.00.
Sanitary Fair, Philadelphia, 1864. sick soldier, etc. Bronze proof. Size 36. 1.50.
Dr. Elisha Kane, bust above Arctic scene; rev., Masonic emblems. Bronze proof. Size 32. 1.25.
Agassiz, bust to right. Bronze proof. Size 29. 1.25.
Washington Irving ; rev., date of birth. Bronze proof. Size 44. 3.50.
A. Thiers, from Philadelphia, 1873. Bronze proof. Size 29. 1.25.
Cyrus W. Field, for Atlantic Cable. Bronze proof. Size 32. 1.00.
Same. White metal proof. .25.
California State Agri. Soc. Award medal. Handsome landscape scene with animals including a large bear, fruits, etc. Very fine. Size 28. Weight 1½ oz. Av. 2.00.
1849. Salem Charitable Mech. Assoc. Hercules has just killed a winged dragon ; boys picking apples from an impossible tree. Size 28. Bronze proof. 1.25.

Centennial Medals.

Centennial Commission Medal. Size 36. Bronze proof in velvet-lined morocco
Lee and Reynolds, Cheyenne Agency, nickel card. Size 20. Buffalo on obverse. Fine and rare. 1.00.
First Steam Coinage at U. S. Mint, Mar. 23, 1836. Cap in rays. Bronze proof. Size 18. .25.
commemorate, etc. Bronze proof, size 37, in case. The handsomest U. S. Centennial Medal. 2.00.
French Centennial. Beautiful head of Liberty ; rev., crossed flags. Beautiful, exceeds anything issued in U S. Bronze proof. Size 32. 2.50.
Brazilian Centennial. Dom Pedro II. (The king that has been lately overthrown). " Exposicao Internaceonal de Philadelphia, 1876." Very fine and rare. 1.50.

Halifax Ferry Token. Steamboat. Bright red proof. 2.00.
White's Farthing, Halifax. Very fine. 5.00.
Francis Mullins & Son. Very fine. 1.00.
Robert Purvis. Uncirculated. .75.
H. Gagnon. Beaver. Extremely fine. Olive. 1.00.
T. S. Brown & Co. Fine. Brown. .35.
Hostermann & Etter. 1815. Fine. .35.
Magdalen Island. Seal and dried codfish. Fine. 1.50.
Montreal and Lachine Railroad Co. Engine and beaver. Large. Extra fine. 3.00.
Nova Scotia and New Brunswick. Ship, "Success" below. Very fine. 5.00.

Ancient and Foreign Gold.

Turkey. Gold. Proof. Size 14. 2.00.
Transylvania. 1657. George Rakoczi II. Ducat. Uncirculated. 6.00.
Salzburg. 1714. Francis Anton. ¼ Ducat. Uncirculated. 2.00.
Nordlingen. 1497. Ducat. The 4 in loop form. One of the earliest dated coins. Very fine. 7.50.
Nurnberg. Pretty little gold coin with lamb and standard. Only 7 cts. in gold. Uncirculated. 1.50.
Guatemala. 1860. 4 Reals. Uncirculated. 1.25.
Spain. 1788. Dollar. About uncirculated. 1.75.
Papal States. 1853. Scudo. Semi-proof. 2.00.
England. 1803. Geo. III. ⅓ Guinea. *Brilliant proof.* 7.50.
England. 1797. Geo. III. ⅓ Guinea. Uncirculated. Brilliant mint bloom. 5.00.
England. 1718. Geo. I. ¼ Guinea. Uncirculated. Brilliant mint bloom. 6.00.
Russia. 3 Roubles. Platinum. About uncirculated. 4.00.
Olmuntz. Wolfgang. ¼ Ducat. Very fine. 1.75.
Roman. (457) Leo I. Rev., Victory holding a cross. Solidus. Very good. 5.00.
(474) Zeno. Rev., Victory holding a cross. Solidus. Very good. 5.00.
(630) Heraclius and son. Rev., cross on pedestal. Solidus. Very fine. 6.00.

Oriental Silver.

Madras. Quarter Pagoda. Tower surrounded by stars; rev., god Vishnu in circle of dots. Fine. 1.50.
Assam. Octagonal Rupee. Very fine. Rare. 2.00.
Burmah. Rupee and ⅛ Rupee. Peacock with spread tail. Very fine. 2.00.
Japan. Itzebue. Uncirculated. .75.
Japan. ¼ Itzebue. Uncirculated. .35.
Siam. Bullet money. Tical. Very fine. 1.25.
Siam. Bullet money. ¼ and ⅛ Tical. Very fine. Each .75.
Persia. ¼ Kran. Sun-lion with sword (dime size). Uncirculated. .50.
Japan. Oblong, one pear shaped, silver dumps, each stamped with characters. They range in size from a pea to ¾ oz. I do not think two sizes are alike. Fine lot. 13 pieces. 12.50.
Japan. Dragon and sun. Yen (Dollar), semi-proof; Sen, proof; 10 and 5 Sen, uncirculated. Lot 3.00.
Siam. Circulars coin with elephant and royal umbrellas. 2, 1, ⅛, 1/16 Tical. About uncirculated. 5.00.
Cambodia. Bird idol. Very fine. Size 8. .50.
Saurashtran, Hindu. Curious figure somewhat resembling a pelican. Size 10. Fine. 1.50.
India. Small dump with idol. Fine. .50.
Java. 1802. Ship. 1-16, ⅛, ¼, ½, 1 Gulden. Uncirculated. Rare set. 7.50.
China. Spanish Dollar covered with Chinese chop marks, a number of which are die-stamps of various designs. 2.50.
Cambodia. Tical. Odd looking bird. Rev., turreted temple. Uncirculated. 5.00.
Madras. Half and Quarter Pagoda. Tower surrounded by stars; rev., God Vishnu

in circle of dots. Value in four languages. Uncirculated. Beautiful pair. 6.00.

Anam. Similar in design to Chinese cash with square hole in centre. Size 20. Uncirculated. Rare. 5.00.

Sandwich Islands. Dime. 1883. Uncirculated. .35.

Mauritius. 1886. 10 Cents. Uncirculated. .35.

Anam. Tu-duk. Tree, shrub and characters. Uncirculated. Size 22. 5.00.

India. Zodiac rupees. Lion and twins. Fine pair. 12.50.

Foreign Silver.

Sweden. 1871. Chas. XV. 4 R. M., 2 R. M., 50, 25, 10 Ore. *Beautiful proofs.* Set for 5.00.

Central America. Dollar. Sun rising behind mountain peaks. But little circulated. Semi-proof. 1.50.

Republic of Columbia. 1820. Dollar. Indian head and pomegranate. Exceptionally fine for this piece. 2.00.

U. S. of Colombia. 1868. Half Dollar. Very fine. 1.00.

Peru. 1833. Liberty standing. Dollar. Barely circulated. Mint lustre. 2.00.

Peru. 1862, 1863, 1864. Callao and Lima. Indian, Liberty in chariot, steamboat. Tokens. ¼ dollar size. Semi-proof. 3 pieces. Lot. 2.50.

Chili. Mining Dollar. Plain planchet with star and 1 P. in sunken counterstamp. Fine. 2.00.

Cordoba. (Argentine Conf.) Dollar. Fort surrounded by seven flags. Very fine. Rare. 5.00.

Caracas. 1811. 2 Reals. Very fine. Rude. .40.

France. Louis XIIII. 1653. Crown. Young head. Very fine. 2.50.

Bavaria. Maximilian II. 1853. ½, 1, 2 Gulden, 1 Thaler. Uncirculated. Mint bloom. Lot 2.50.

Neapolitan Republic. Liberty standing. Year 7. Fine. 2.50.

Sandwich Islands. Kalakaua I. Dime. Brilliant proof. .50.

Japan. Dragon. Yen, 50, 20, 10, 5 sen. Uncirculated. Lot 2.50.

Sierra Leone. 1791. Dollar. Lion. Sharp, uncirculated, proof surface. 7.50.

Hayti. 1881. Gourde (Dollar), 20, 10 cts. Beautiful design. Brilliant mint lustre. Set 2.50.

New Grenada. 1847. 2, 8 Reals. Very fine. Scarce. Pair 2.50.

Bolivia. 1884. Dime. Br. Proof. .50.

Sardinia. 1859. Victor Emmanuel. 5 Lire. Brilliant mint lustre. 1.50.

Mexico. 1866. Maxmilian. Dollar and half. Barely circulated. Pair 2.50.

1867. Peru. Dollar. Seated Liberty. Uncirculated. 1.25.

1877. Chili. Dollar. Condor. Uncirculated. 1.50.

1817. Spain. Ferd. VII. Dollar. Counterstamped for Brazil. Extremely fine. 1.25.

Tranquebar. Dump with idol. Very fine. .65.

France. Napoleon III. 1852. ½, 1 fr. Uncirculated. 2 pcs. Lot. .50.

Assam. Octagonal rupee, curious dragon at bottom, extremely fine. 2.00.

Kempten. Bust of the Bishop. Bracteates. Size 14. Uncirculated. 10 pcs. Lot 2.50.

Lille. Marshal's batons crowned, rev., mailed arm with sword. "Non sine numine," necessity money, very fine, size 19. 1.50.

Small bracteates. 25 pcs. Lot. 1.00.

Mexico. 1812. Vargas dollar. Fair (never found better). 1.25.

Central America. Sun rising behind mountain peaks. 1, 2 reals. Pair. .50.

Guatemala. 1808. Ferd. VII. Proclamation 2 reals. Fort on shield. Very good. 2.00.

Guatemala. Sept. 24, 1812. 2 reals. Open book in rays, arms of Guatemala. Fine. Pierced. .50.

Berne. 1795. Dollar. Swiss soldier. Rev., Bear on shield. *Proof.* A beauty. 5.00.

Canton Zurich. 1813. Dollar. Semi proof. A beauty. 5.00.
Canton Luzerne. 18 4. Dollar. Swiss soldier. *Proof*. A beauty. 5.00.
France. 1844. Louis Philippe. 5 Francs. Br. proof. 2.50.
1789. Louis XVI. Crown. About uncirculated. 3.00.
Louis XV. and XVI. Tokens. 1735, 1741, etc. ½, ¼ (3) Crowns. Ship under
    full sail, Justice with scales, tree growing, etc. Fine. 4 pcs. 2.50.
Republic. 1849. 20, 50c., 1, 5 Francs. Uncirculated. Mint bloom. Lot. 1.75.
Republic. 1852. Louis Napoleo 1 Bonaparte. 50c., 1, 5 Francs. Uncirculated.
    Mint bloom. 1.75.

Silver Coins of Great Britain.

Early British Tetradrachm. Idiotic head; rev., shadowy horseman on colossal
    horse. Very fine. 6.00.
Early British Didrachm. Lines, pellets and dots. Fine and curious. 2.00.
Ethelred II. 978. Holding sceptre, large cross on rev. Silver penny. Very
    fine. 2.00.
Edward the Confessor. 1042. Silver penny. Bust with sceptre. BRAND ON
    WAERINE. Very fine. 2.00.
William the Conqueror. 1066. Silver penny. Fine. 2.00. Good. 1.50.
Henry II. 1154. Silver penny. Good. 1.00.
Richard I. 1189. Pictaine silver penny. Very good. 1.50.
Henry III. 1216. Silver penny. Very good. .50.
Edward I. 1272. Silver penny. Fine. .50.
Edward I. 1272. Groat. Good. .75.
Edward II. 1307. Silver penny. Fine. .75.
Edward III. 1327. Groat. Good. .75. Half Groat. Good. .75.   •
Henry V. 1413. Groat. Fine. 1.00.
Henry VI. 1422. Groat. Very fine. 1.00.
Edward IV. 1461. Halfpenny. Very good. .75.
Henry VII. 1485. Groat. Front face. Fine. 1.25.
Henry VII. 1485. Groat. Side view. Extremely fine. 2.00.
Henry VII. 1485. Half Groat. Issued by Archbishop Morton. Good. 1.50.
Henry VIII. 1509. Groat. Side view. Fine. .75.
Henry VIII. 1509. Groat. Front face. Fine. 1.00. Good. .50.
Edward VI. 1547. Broad Shilling. Very fine. 2.00. Fine. 1.50.
Mary. 1553. Groat. Very fine. 2.00. Good. 1.25.
Mary. 1553. Groat. Bust of Mary. Legend " Philip and Maria." Fine. 2.00.
Elizabeth. 1601. Crown. Very good, fine for this piece. Very rare. 20.00.
Elizabeth. 1562. Milled Sixpence. Extremely fine. 2.00.
Elizabeth. 1602. Hammered Sixpence. Very fine. .75.
James I. 1603. Half Crown. King on horseback. Very fair. 1.25.
James I. 1603. Shilling. Fine. 1.25. Very good. .75.
James I. 1603. Sixpence. Fine. .75. Good. .50.
Charles I. 1625. Shilling. Fine. .75. Good. .50.
Charles I. Threepence, Welsh. Halfpenny. Rose. Very fine. Pair. 1.50.
Commonwealth. 1653. Twopence. Fine. 1.00.
Commonwealth. 1653. Penny. Fine. 1.00.
Commonwealth. 1653. Halfpenny. Fine. Rare. 1.50.
Oliver Cromwell. 1658. Crown. A beautiful uncirculated specimen, the crack in
    the die scarcely showing. 50.00.
Oliver Cromwell. 1658. Crown. Only the barest touch of circulation on most
    prominent parts of obverse. 30.00. Another, fine. 20.00.
Oliver Cromwell. 1658. Half Crown. *Brilliant proof*. Said to be the finest
    known. 75.00.
Oliver Cromwell. 1658. Half Crown. Extremely fine. 20.00. Very good.
    10 00.
Oliver Cromwell. 1658. Shilling. Barely circulated. 15.00. Fine. 10.00.
Charles II. 1665. Pattern farthing in silver. Uncirculated. 3.50.

James II. 1687. Crown. Uncirculated. Mint bloom. 15.00.
James II. 1687. 40 Shilling piece. **Extremely fine.** 7.50.
James II. Maundy Set. Extremely fine. 2.50.
William and Mary. 1693. Half Crown. Rev., 4 shields, monogram W M and
  date in angles. Very good. 1.50.
William and Mary. 1689. 3 and 4 pence. Very fine. Pair 1.00.
William III. 1698. Half Crown. Uncirculated, some proof surface. 4.00.
Anne. 1707. Crown. Rev., roses and plumes in the angles. Fine. 3.00.
George II. Maundy Set. 1730-1743. Uncirculated. 2.00.
George III. Northumberland Shilling. 1763. Proof. 7.50.
George III. 1787. Sixpence and Shilling. Uncirculated. Semi-proof. Pair 1.25.
1804. Bank of England. Dollar. Very fine. 2.00.
1804. Bank of Ireland. Dollar. Fine. Rare. 5.00.
George III. 1818. Pistrucci Crown. St. George and the dragon. Proof. 7.50.
George III. 1819. Pistrucci Crown. St. George and the dragon. Proof. 7.50.
George III. 1763. Maundy Set. Uncirculated. 1 50.
George III. 1800. Maundy Set. Small head, large bust. Proofs except 3 pence
  which is 1795, uncirculated. 2.00.
George III. 1818. Maundy Set. Bull head. Uncirculated. 1.50.
George IV. 1823. Maundy Set. Proofs. 2.00.
Victoria. Gothic Crown. Smooth edge. Brilliant proof. 25.00.
Scotland. Robert II. 1370. Groat. Very good. 1.50.
Mary. "Nonsunt." M. crowned. Rev., "IAM NON SVNT DVO SED VNA
  CARO." Good. 2.00.
James VI. 1594. Thistle Mark. Bust of James; rev., thistle. Fine. 5.00.
James VI. 1601. Thistle Mark. Shield; rev., thistle. Fine. 5.00.
Ireland. 1723. Wood Sixpence. Similar in design to the Wood halfpence, which
  were rejected in Ireland and then extensively circulated in America. Ex-
  tremely fine and *excessively rare.* 25.00.

Foreign Coppers.

Where more than one piece is given on a line, the price is for all and not per piece.
Antigua. 1836. Palm tree. Farthing. Fine. .50.
Argentine Confederation. Head of Liberty. 1, 2 Centavos. Uncirculated. Bright
  red. .50.
Andora. 1873. 10 Centimes. Proof. The only coin of this little republic. .25.
Bolivia. 1883. 1, 2 Centavos. Proof. .50.
British Honduras. 1885. Cent. Uncirculated. Bright red. .25.
Barbadoes. Penny. Negro head and pineapple. Fine. .75. Good. .50.
Barbadoes. Penny and Halfpenny. Neptune in car. Also, Penny. Pineapple.
  Set of 3 pcs. Proofs. Handsome. 15.00.
Bermuda. 1793. Penny. Extremely fine. Light olive. .75.
Bahama. Halfpenny. Ship sailing. Uncirculated. .50.
Bulgaria. 1879-1887. 10 Centimes. Uncirculated. Set of 5 pieces. .50.
Byzantine (Constantinople before the Turkish occupation). Cup-shaped. Fine. 1.00
  Good. .50.
Congo Free States. 1, 2, 5, 10 Centimes. Round hole in centre. Uncirculated.
  Bright red. Set for .35.
Cambodia. Norodom I. 1860. 5, 10 Centesimos. Beautiful proofs. .50.
Cyprus. 1, ½, ¼ Piastre. Uncirculated. Bright red. 1.00.
Ceylon. 1815. ½, 1, 2 Stivers. Elephant. Very good and fine. 2.00.
Carthagena. Indian under tree. ¼, 2 R. Very good. .75.
Cape of Good Hope. 1889. Penny. Brilliant proof. .50.
Caracas. ¼ R. Very fine. .25.
Dominica. 1848. ¼ R. Very fine. .25.
Dominica. 1877. Centavo. Uncirculated. .25.
Dominica. 1877. 2½ Centavos. Nickel. Proof. .25.
Dutch East Indies. 6 St. 4¾ inches long. VI—St at each end on both sides.
  Very fine. Excessively rare. 15.00.

England. 1714. Anne. Farthing. Bust; rev., Britannia seated, 1714. Uncir culated. Glossy light brown color. 15.00.
Geo. III. 1797. Twopenny. Weight 2 oz. Uncirculated. 2.50. Fine. 1.50. Good. 1.00. Fair. .50.
1797 Geo. III. Penny. Weight 1 oz. Uncirculated. 1.50.
1797. Coventry Halfpennies. Arms of Coventry; elephant with castle on back, tiger above. Revs, different buildings in Coventry—St. Mary's Hall, St. John's Church, White Friars, Grey Friars Steeple, Trinity Church, etc. Bronze proofs. 15 pcs. 1.pt, 10 00.
Ecuador. 1872. 1, 2 Centavos. Very good. Rare. 1.50.
Ecuador. 1884. ½, 1 Centavos. Nickel. Very rare. Very fine pair. 2.50.
Guatemala. 1871. Centavo. Mountain peaks. Good. .50.
Greece. Head. 1, 2, 5, 10 Lepta. Uncirculated. Bright red. 1.00.
Guiana (Spanish). Lion; rev., castle. Very good. Rude. .50.
Guernsey. 1, 2, 4, 8 Doubles. 1889. Uncirculated. Bright red. .50.
Hayti. 1877. Mercury head. 20 Cent. Proof. .25.
Hong Kong. Cent and Mil. Uncirculated. Bright. .30.
Island of Sumatra. Fine. .25.
Ionian Isles. ¼, ½, 1, 2 Obolo. Fine set. 2.00.
Isle of Man. 1786. George III. Penny and Halfpenny. This and the following have the three legs joined on reverse. Fine. .75.
1813. Head of Geo. III. Uncirculated. Light olive. 1.50. Nearly as choice. 1.00.
Island of Ceylon. Vidschaya Bahu II. 1186-1187. Same. Massa. Very fine. 1.00.
Bhuvanaika Bahu. 1296-1314. Same. Massa. Very fine. 1.00.
Ireland. Gun Money of James II. A remarkably large collection, containing nearly all the varieties. In condition from fair to about uncirculated; many are very fine, the best a former owner could find out of hundreds examined. Half Crowns. 1689: Jan., Mar., July, Aug., Sep., Dec. 1690: Mar., Apr., May (large and small), June, July. 1690: King on horseback. Shillings. 1689: Jan., Feb., Mar., July, Aug., Aug't, Sep'r, Sep't, 9, Oct., 10, Nov., Dec. 1690: Apr., May, may, June, Sep. Sixpences. 1689: Jan., Feb., June, July, Aug., Sep'r, 7ber, Dec. 39 pieces. 25.00.
Java. ½ St. Fine. .35.
Java. 1 Stiver. Without date. Thick dump. Fine. .75.
Java. 1802. 2 Stubers. Oblong bar. Very good. 1.50.
Java. 1818. 1, 2 Stubers. Oblong bar. Very good. Each, 1.50.
Japan. Tempo. Oblong. (See cut.) Fine. .15.
Liberia. 1833. Negro, tree and ship. Uncirculated. Brown. .50.
Liberia. 1847. Cent. Palm tree. Extremely fine. .50.
Liberia. 1862. Cent and Two Cents. Fine. .75.
Liberia. 1862. Two Cents. Proof. 1.25. Extremely fine. .50.
Monaco. 1838. 5, 10 Centimes. Br. proof. .50.
Malacca. "Cock of the Walk" (See cut). Very fine. .35.
Meysore. Elephant. Thick dump. 5 Cash. Very fine. .50.
Meysore. Lion. Thick dump. 20 Cash. Very fine. .75.
Mexico. Chihuahua. 1860. Liberty seated. ¼ R. Very good. .50.
Chihuahua. 1846. ¼ R. Indian. Fine. .60. Very good. .35.
Sinaloa. Head of Liberty. ¼ R. Fine. .50. Good. .25.
Zacatecas. Quartilla. Temple and angel. Very good. 1.00.
Zacatecas. Octavo. Temple and angel. Very good. 1.00.
Mexico. 1864. Centavo of Maxmilian. Fine. 1.00. Good. .50.
Orange Free States. 1888. Penny. Brilliant proof. .35.
Persia. Fath Ali Schah. 1797-1834. 1½ Bisti. Rabbit. Very good. 1.00.
Same ruler. 1½ Bisti. Sun-lion. Fine. 1.00.
Portugal. Maria II. 5 Reis. Uncirculated. Bright red. .25.
Patagonia. Orille-Antoine I. 1874. 2 Centavos. Proof. .25.
Portuguese Africa. ½, 1 Macuta. Very fine. 1 25.
Papal States. Pius IX. 4 Soldi. Bright. .50. Extra fine, olive. .35.

Papal States. Gregory XVI. and Pius IX. Baiocco. Uncirculated. Bright. .75.
Poland. 1831. 3 Grosze. Uncirculated. Brilliant red. .25.
Roman Republic. 40, 4 Baiocchi. Base silver. Very fine and uncirculated. 1.50.
Roman Republic. 3 Baiocchi. Uncirculated. Bright red. 1.00.
Roumania. 5, 10 Bani. Extremely fine. .50.
Sierra Leone. Prowling lion. 1791. Cent. Bronze proof. 1.00.
Sarawak. Cent. Bright. 1.00. Fine. .50.
Sandwich Islands. Kamehameha III. Hapi Haneri. Uncirculated. Bright red.
   .75. Fine. .50.
Siberia. 1764. Set of 10, 5, 3, 2, 1, ½ Kopec, the latter (usually catalogued as ¼
   Kopec) very scarce. All with Sable Foxes except the ½ Kopec. Very
   fine. 7.50.
South Africa. 1890. Penny. Br. proof. .25.
Sweden. Large Or. Size 30. 1685. Fine. 1.00.
States of Jersey. 1888. 1–12, 1–24 Sh. Uncirculated. Bright red. .35.
Sicily. 1849. Ferd. II. ½. 1, 2 Tornese. Uncirculated. Bright red. .75.
Sicily under Napoleon. Head of Jerome Napoleon. 3 Grana. Good. .75.
Strasburg. Siege Decime. 1814–1815. L and N crowned. Fine. Pair. .75.
St. Helena. Halfpenny. Very good. .20.
Sweden. Plate money. One Daler. 1745. Very fine. 7.50.

War Medals.

United States. Silver medal presented to William Bolt, by City of New York
   for the war with Mexico. Arms of New York, rev., typical female pointing to city and harbor—Cerro Gordo—Chapultepec—Cherubusco—Vera
   Cruz. Brilliant proof. Size 32. Weight 2 oz. Av. 6.00.
Silver medal presented by South Carolina to Palmetto Regiment, Mexican War.
   Palmetto tree; rev., troops landing from boats. Silver. Very fine. Size
   31. 7.50.
" Death to traitors;" medal of the Iron Brigade, N. Y. Vol's; white metal, ribbon.
   attached. Good. Size 24. 1.00.
West Virginia. Liberty crowning a soldier, 1861–1865. Copper. Uncirculated.
   3.00. Very good. 1.50.
Anhalt. Shield of arms crowned ; rev., bear walking on wall. Order of "Albert
   the Bear," bronze proof. Size 20. 1.25.

The following English medals all have head of Victoria on obverse and are silver of size 24 unless
otherwise described.

England. Army of Punjab. Rev., soldiers surrendering to mounted British officers.
   1849. Two bars, " Mooltan and Goojerat," ribbon attached. Very fine.
   6.00.
" Northwest Frontier." Rev., Victory crowning a naked warrior. Bar, " North-
   west Frontier," ribbon attached. Very fine. 5.00.
" Pegu." Same reverse. Bar, " Pegu." Very fine. 3.50.
" Umbeyla." Same reverse. Bar, " Umbeyla." Very fine. 5.00.
Crimea. Four bars. "Alma, Balaklava, Inkermann, Sebastapol," ribbon attached.
   Very fine. 15.00.
Crimea. Rev., flying Victory placing wreath on warrior in Roman costume,
   " Crimea" in field. Three bars, " Sebastopol, Inkermann, Alma," ribbon
   attached. Very fine. 10.00.
Same. One bar, " Sebastopol," ribbon attached, very fine. 4.00. Another without
   bar but with swivel and ribbon, very fine. 3.00. Another, no bar or rib-
   bon, very fine. 2.50.
India, 1857–58. Rev., Una and the lion. Bar, " Delhi," ribbon attached. Semi-
   proof. Rare. 6.00.
India, 1857–58. Same reverse. Bar, Lucknow. Very fine. 4.00.
India, 1857–58. Same reverse. Swivel and ribbon. Very fine. 3.00.
India, 1857–58. Same reverse. Bar, "Central India." Very fine. 4.00.

India, 1857–58. Same reverse. Two bars, "Lucknow," "Defense of Lucknow," ribbon attached. Fine. 6.00.

Baltic, 1854–55. Rev., Britannia seated, two fortresses in background. Bar and ribbon. Proof. 3.50.

China. Rev., trophy of arms, flags, etc., "China" below. Two bars, "Pekin 1860 and Taku Forts 1860," ribbon attached. Fine. 5.00

South Africa. Rev., Lion and bush, "South Africa" above. Bar, "1879," ribbon attached. Very fine. 3.50.

New Zealand. Head crowned, veil falling down behind; rev., wreath, "New Zealand Virtutis Honor." Ornamented bar and ribbon. Very fine. 4.00.

Abyssinia. Crowned and veiled head in centre of large star, between the points, "Abyssinia;" rev., name of wearer in wreath. Crown and ring with ribbon above. Semi proof. Size 22. 5.00.

Veiled head of Victoria; rev., a number of semi-nude Ashantees fighting in bush with infantry. Bar and ribbon. Very fine. 3.50.

Egypt. Soudan. Bust of Queen; rev., sphinx. Bar, "El teb-tamaai," ribbon attached. Fine proof. 6.00.

Egypt. Same design. Bar, "The Nile, 1884–85," ribbon attached. Fine proof. 6.00.

Egypt. Same design. Bar, "Suakim, 1885." Proof. 6.00.

Egypt. Same design. Bar, "Tel-el kebir," ribbon attached. Fine proof. 6.00.

Bust of Queen: rev., sphinx, 1882, Egypt. Bar, "Tel-el-kebir," ribbon attached. Officers' medal. Semi proof. Size 12. 3.00.

Afghanistan. Rev., elephant artillery Bar "Ali Musjid," ribbon attached. Semi-proof. 6.00. Another, plain bar, with ribbon. Proof. 4.00.

Afghanistan. Same design. Bar, "Ahmed Khel," ribbon attached. Fine proof. 6.00.

Persia. Rev., Victory crowning Roman warrior Bar, "Persia." Fine proof. 6.00.

Syria. 1848. Rev., Britannia seated on hippocampus. Bar, "Syria," ribbon attached. Brilliant proof. 6.00.

Coat of Arms: rev., "For long service and good conduct." Bar with ribbon. Proof. 4.00.

France. Napoleon III. Expedition to China, 1860. Head. Rev., names of battles. Ribbon with Chinese characters attached. Silver. Size 20. Unused. 3.50.

Same. Officers' size. With ribbon. Unused. Size 11. 2.50.

Same. Unused. Size 7. 1.50.

Napoleon III. For Mexican campaign. 1862–1863. Silver. Very fine. Ribbon attached. Size 20 2.50.

Republic. Expedition to China, 1883–1885. Rev., names of battles. Silver. Size 20. Unused. 3.00.

Saxe-Gotha-Altenburg. The Altenburg rose; rev., ducal crown. Bronze. Very fine. Size 27. 1.00.

Turkey. For Crimea, 1855. Trophy of cannon, etc.; rev., cipher of Abdul Medjid. Silver. Size 24. Very fine. 2.00.

Numismatic Books and Pamphlets.

"Early Half Dimes," Harold P. Newlin, 1883. Full descriptions of the varieties of the early dates and also an interesting article on the whereabouts of all the known 1802 Half Dimes. Fine paper with broad margins. New. Edition very limited. Illustrated with plates. Cloth, 1.00. Paper (no plates) reduced to .25.

Madden's History of Jewish coinages. Many illustrations. 350 pages. Half morocco. New and uncut. 5.00.

Atlas Numismatique du Canada. Jos. Le Roux. 1883. 40 pages, with illustrations of all the 220 Canadian coins. Letter press in English and French. A valuable work. Paper covers. 1.00.

Silver coins of England. Henry. 1878. 48 pages. Illustrated pamphlet. .35.

Numisgraphics or a list of sale catalogues. Atinnelli, 1876. 134 pages. Half morocco. Annotated. Rare. 2.00.

Haseltine's "Paper Money of the Colonies." Illustrated. Pamphlet. 5 plates.
  Reduced to .15.
Haseltine's "Confederate Notes and Bonds." .50.
"Das Romische Ass." German. 24 pages. 6 plates. .35.
The Naturalist's Directory. Cassino. 1886. 4801 names. 1.00.
Coins, medals and seals. W. C. Prime. 114 plates. 292 pages. Cloth. New
  York, 1861. 3.50.
Coins of the Grand Master of Malta. R. Morris, Boston, 1884. 6 plates. 70 pages
  Cloth. 1.50.
Historia Numorum. A Manual of Greek Numismatics by Barclay V. Head, Assistant
  Keeper of the Department of Coins and Medals in the British Museum.
  1887. Hundreds of illustrations. 818 pages. Half morocco. By far the
  best work of its class ever issued. 12.50.
New Varieties of Gold and Silver Coins, etc. Eckfeldt and Dubois. Phila., 1850.
  Covers loose. Illustrated. Contains about 50 to 75 cts. worth of real gold
  fastened to page 45 illustrating metals. 1.50.
Marvin's Masonic Medals. 17 plates. Also, accurate descriptions of 744 medals.
  Heavy paper. The standard American publication. 350 pages. New.
  10.00.
Conder. "An Arrangement of Provincial Coins, Tokens, etc.," by James Con-
  der. Ipswich, 1798. 12mo, 330 pp., 3 plates, half morocco, clean.
  The standard authority on its series. 12.50.
Philips. The Paper Currency of the American Colonies. Roxbury, published
  by W. Elliott Woodward, 1865. Small 4to, 264 pp., unbound. 2 vols.
  Scarce. 5.00.
Satterlee. Presidential Medals and Tokens. New York, 1862. 8vo, 84 pp.,
  cloth. Loose photo. of author. Scarce. 2.50. Same, paper cover. 2.00.
Bolen's Medals, Cards and Fac-similes, an accurate Catalogue of, by E. L. John-
  son. 8vo, cloth. Springfield, 1882. 1 00.
Descriptive Catalogue of the Seavey Collection. Bought by Loring G Parmelee.
  8 plates of photographs. 8vo, half morocco. Privately printed. 4 00.
Coins of the World. 12 fac-simile plates. 12mo. In paper cover. Philadelphia, 1849. 1.00.
Coin Book. With 16 plates of figures. 8vo. Philadelphia, 1872. 2.00.
Du Bois, W. E. Brief Account of the U. S. Mint Collection. Plate. Small
  12mo, half roan. Rare. Philadelphia, 1846. 2.00.
Eckfeldt and Du Bois. A Manual of Gold and Silver Coins of all Nations, struck
  within the past century. With engravings. 4to, cloth. Philadelphia,
  1842. 2.50.
New Varieties of Gold and Silver Coins, Counterfeits, and Bullion. Second
  edition. 8vo. New York, 1851. .50.
Evans, G. G. Illustrated History of the United States Mint, with a complete
  description of American Coinage. Illustrated with phototypes, steel-
  plate portraits and wood cuts, etc. New and revised edition. 8vo,
  paper. Philadelphia, 1885. .50.
Hawkins, Ed. The Silver Coins of England arranged and described, with re-
  marks on British Money previous to the Saxon Dynasties. 47 plates.
  8vo, half roan. London, 1841. 4.00.
Haym, N. F. Thesauri Britannici pars altera, seu Museum Nummarium com-
  plexum Numos Græcos et Latinos omnis metalli. 51 plates of coins
  4to, old calf. 1765. 3 00.
Henry, J. The Series of English Coins in Copper, Tin and Bronze. Small 4to.
  London, 1879. 1.00
Humphreys, H. N. The Coinage of the British Empire. Illustrated by fac
  similes of the coins of each period, worked in gold, silver and copper.
  8vo. London, 1855. 4.00.
Manual of Roman Coins. With 21 plates. 8vo. London, 1865. 2.50.
Introduction a la Connoissance des Médailles. par C. Patin. 16mo, vellum,
  sheep. Paris, 1667. .75.

Tristan, l. Commentaires Historiques—les Vies, eloges et censures des Empereurs, Imperatrices, Cæsars et Tyrans de l'Empire Romain, le tout illustré de l'exacte explication des revers enigmatiques de plusieurs centaines de médailles, etc. Many fine copper-plates. Folio, old calf. Paris, 1635. 3.50.

Wharton, J. Memorandum concerning Small Money and Nickel Alloy Coinage. With illustrations. Pamphlet. .75.

Another. Second Edition. 1.00.

Woodward, W. Elliot. A List of Washington Memorial Medals. Two fine portraits. 8vo, half morocco. Only 50 copies printed. 1865. 5.00.

Snelling, T. The Doctrine of Gold and Silver Computations. With tables and copper-plates. 8vo, half roan. London, 1766. 1.00.

History of the Bills of Credit or Paper Money issued by New York. John H. Hickcox. 103 pages. Large paper, uncut. Albany, 1866. 3.50.

Varieties of the Copper Issues of the United States Mint in the year 1794. Edward Maris, M. D. Philadelphia, 1869. 2.00.

Addison's Dialogues on Medals. 8 plates. 1.00.

Medals by Giovanni Cavino (the Paduan). Richard H. Lawrence. Illustrated. Privately printed. New York, 1883. 1.25.

The Coin Collector's Manual. H. Noel Humphreys. Over 150 illustrations on wood and steel. 726 pages. Half morocco. London, 1871. 6.00.

Medals Awarded by Foreign Societies to Kane, Hayes and Hall. Prof. J. E. Nourse, U. S. N. 1 plate. Cloth. 1876. Rare. 1.25.

Catalogue of Parmelee sale. Unpriced. .50.

Another. Priced and bound in cloth. 1.50.

Catalogue of Robt. C. Davis Collection. Priced and bound in cloth. 1.50.

Descriptive Catalogue of a Cabinet of Roman Family Coins, belonging to the Duke of Northumberland, by Rear-Admiral William Henry Smith. Large 4to. Cloth. 323 pages. Privately printed. London, 1856. 7.50.

Traite Des Monnaies D'Or et D'Argent. Par Pierre-Frederic Bonneville. 268 pgs. Folio. Uncut. Paris, 1806. Beautiful copy of a desirable work containing a great many coin plates with illustrations of hundreds of coins. 5.00.

Priced catalogues of W. Elliot Woodward. Includes Sheldon, 1863–4, C. Wyllis Betts, Jencks, Parmolee, McCoy (very rare and desirable), Chambers, Finotti, Brooks & Shurtleff (large paper unpriced dup, of last two), J. N. T. Levick, 6th, 7th, 8th and other early sales. Rare and desirable lot. 21 pcs. 5.00.

Curiosities.

Knight of Pythias sword. Handsome steel scabbard and mountings. Knights, Pilgrims, Eagles, etc. Very fine and desirable. Probably made for an officer and cost about $30. Uninjured by use. In buckskin cover. 10.00.

Massive brown agate paper weight, in shape of a seal and handle, cut from one piece. Very handsome and valuable. 5¾ inches long, 2¾ inches wide at top. 5.00.

Seal. Similar. Red agate. 2⅛ inches long. Handsome. 2.50.

Marble paper weight. "Appian Way," near Ravenna, Italy. .75.

Egyptian scarabeus. Very fine. 1.50.

Olive wood pipe. Liberty bell design. New. .50.

Japan. Native painted photo. on glass in case. Very odd. 1.00.

Japan. Opium pipe. New. .75.

Piece of gold ore, oval, polished ready for mounting as a breast pin. Size 26. 5.00.

Aztec Idol, carved from pumice stone, prehistoric, very fine specimen, dug from mound near Durango, Mexico. 15x9x7 inches. Very desirable. 100.00.

Hindoo Idol. Fine white marble. Old. 16 x 9½ in. 25.00.

Old Japanese. God of Plenty. Very odd. Bronze. 6 x 4 in. 10.00.

Old Japanese. Dog Foy on stump. Bronze. 4 x 4 in. 10.00.
Agate egg. Full size of a hen's egg. Very handsome. 1.50.
Paper weight. Glass. View of foreign building. 3 inches. .50.
Ostrich egg. South Africa. Fine large specimen. 2.50.
Indian doe-skin slipper. Fancy bead work. Very fine. 1.00.
Pottery vase and ball stopper from Cyprus. Old and valuable. 2.00.
Ancient bronze statuette. Venus. 2½ in. From Syria. 3.00.
Ancient bronze statuette. Curious animal. 1½ in. From Syria. 2.00.
Ancient Roman spearhead, iron, 3½ in. From German Mound. 2.00.
Terra Vert Ancient Egyptian ornaments, Lion, Anubias, etc. 5 pcs. Lot for 7.50.
Plumes of the Egret or White Crane, snow white, 22 in., Florida. 2.00.
Skin of Mottled Crane, very fine, 27 in., Florida. 1.50.
Curious polished stone, natural scene resembling a river and bank with trees and
    foliage. 10½ in. 5.00.
Remarkable clay idol from Guatemala. Human figure with tail. Head broken
    from body (has been mended), and part of legs missing. Curious and rare.
    2.50.
Florida sea-beans. 14 pcs. .75.
Gourd Dish. From Peruvian mound. Fine. 1.00.
Brazil. Nut-case filled with nuts. 4x4. 2.00.
Curious bark writing in native India characters, 3 fine specimens, and a piece of
    tappa cloth. 4 pcs. 1.00.
Pair of very old galoshes. 1.50.
Handsome polished tiger-eye ball, suitable for cane or umbrella handle. 1¾ in. in
    diameter. 1.00.
Remarkable old mortar and pestle. The mortar is dated 1694, and has odd dragon
    head handles. 10.00.
Pair of handles from very old desk, ram's head with ring in mouth. Bronze. 1.00.
Apache horn spoon. 9 in. in length. 4 in. wide. 1.50.
Wooden vases. 5½ in. high. Made from the Great Elm on Boston Common. 2
    pcs. 1.00.
Geode, Ill. 4½ in. wide, 2 in. high. Nice specimen. 1.50.
Amethyst crystals. Hungary. 4x3½ in. 1.50.
Peacock Brass Incense Burner. 14 in. high. Beautifully carved with Persian
    figures. A rare Persian ornament. 15.00.
Bowl. Brass. Persia. A beautiful, rare and valuable specimen. 10 in. in diame-
    ter, 6 in. deep. The sides beautifully ornamented with procession of 12
    odd figures of priests and animals. 10.00.
Mounted lens (2), each 2 in., on stand. 1.00.
Olive wood seal top. .25.
Fine specimen of opal in matrix. Mexico. 1.50.
Gold ore, oval polished specimens, once set in sleeve-buttons, contain considerable
    gold. Size 9. 4 pcs. 5.00.
Curious match-safe, form of beetle. 4 in. .50.
Brass candlesticks. Assortment of designs, all polished. 43 pcs. 15 00.
Brass candlestick, snuffers and tray, polished. Old and desirable. 3.50.
Very old paper-snapper, brass dragon. 5 in. 1.00.
Bone spoons, very old, 6 inches. 4 pcs. 1.50.
Bone two pronged fork, very old. 6½ in. 1.00.
Very old powder-flask. 2.00.
Very old knife, four broad blades, three with crescent projections to cut button-holes,
    handle about 1½ inch at bottom and only ½ inch at top. Curious. 2.50.
Very old wooden spoon, large bowl, elaborately carved handle; evidently a high-
    priced soup-spoon. 9 in. 1.50.
Beautiful necklace of 50 handsome large Brazilian agate beads, finely matched in
    size and markings. 5.00.
Curious carved ivory clenched hands (tops of old seals). 4 pcs. 2.00.
South Sea Islander's wooden spear. In two pieces (made that way). 32 inches.
    1.50.

Small figure of Napoleon, lead. very old. .50.
Ivory chessmen from Siam. Old. 3 pcs. 1.50.
Egypt. Goddess of Evil, Taur. 3500 years old. Hyena headed goddess with big
    feet. Fine. 2¾ inches. Very rare. 10.00.
Antique lamp, Roman, of the kind used in Biblical times. Very fine specimen. 5.00.
Paper cutter. Brass. India. Double god at end. 9½ inches. 2.50.
Whale's tooth. Polished specimen. 6¾ in. 2.00.
Hammer. Walrus tusk head. 1.00.
Marline spike. Walrus tusk. 12 in. 1.50.
Water-works, Philadelphia (at Broad and Market, where public buildings now
    stand). Breakfast plate. Black. 3.00.
Porcelain Cup and Saucer. Royal Sevres. From the set of King Louis Phil-
    ippe of France at the Chateau Fontainebleau. Marked with the king's
    monogram and name of chateau. Very desirable. 25.00.

Collection of Proof Sets.

1859–1892. A collection of 35 Proof Sets, inclusive of both sets of 1873 ("Old"
    and " New " style) in choice condition. Cheap at 150.00.

Diamonds, Jewelry, etc.

Gold Ring. Fine white diamond, about one carat. A pretty little sparkler.
    Cost 85.00. 50.00.
Handsome moon-stone pin, the stone finely carved with a moon-face. Sur-
    rounded by four pretty little diamonds, size usually selling at 10 to 15
    dollars each, retail. Finely mounted with gold setting and pin. 37.50.
Diamond pin. The centre stone is about one carat, eight diamonds surround-
    ing it. All are guaranteed genuine diamonds, but of the poorer qual-
    ity, almost black and irregularly cut. Only good as samples. 10 00.
Antique Gold Beads. Large string. Weight in gold about ½ oz. Troy. 10.00.
Pair of Antique Gold Ear-rings. Pendant form. 5.00.
Pair of Antique Gold Ear-rings. Oval. 5.00.
Antique Silver Cream Pitcher and Sugar Bowl. Sterling silver. Have not had
    weighed accurately, but from scales tried on they weighed about 35 oz.
    Troy. 60.00.
Gold Watch. About 100 years old. Running order. Fine antique face. 15.00.
Silver Bull Eye Watch. Antique. 5.00.
Gold Bracelet. Form of a snake. Two diamonds for eyes. 20.00.
Sleeve Buttons. Pair of curious Japanese. Pair of quails, flowers, etc., on
    each in gold on rubber. 7.50.
Large Oval Medallion or Breast pin. Cupid and dove painted on porcelain and
    mounted in handsome gold frame. The painting is superb, and pro-
    nounced by several artists to whom it was shown as elegant work.
    Cost 50.00. 30.00.
Mary, Queen of Scots. Exquisite little painting on porcelain. 5.00.
Gold Padlock and Key. Suitable for watch-chain or bracelet. 3 50.
Handsome string of 33 pretty "cat-eyes." 7 50.
Madonna and Child. Medallion or breast-pin. Beautifully painted and in
    magnificent carved ivory frame. 10.00.
Raphael's Madonna and Child and the well known Cherubs. Painted on por-
    celain in gold frames. Breast-pin and ear-rings (the cherubs are the
    ear-rings). Set 12.50.
Napoleon the Great. Pretty miniature on porcelain in gold frame. Old. 10.00.
Mosaic. Oval. St. Peter's at Rome. Very pretty. 5.00.
Antique Watch Key. Bead work. Very old. 2 50.
Antique Watch Key. Equally old. Large oval stone in centre. 2.00.
Bracelet. 6 oval female heads finely carved out of as many different shades of
    lava. 2 50.

Byzantine Madonna. Very old. The crown on heads of Mary and child Jesus, as well as a very elaborate frame work surrounding, is made of the finest possible silk filigree work interspersed with stones (some may be gems), including some genuine pearls. 75.00.

Japanese Stone Carving. The Philosopher. Handsome. 12.50.

Bamboo Carving. Lion and cub resting under a tree. Extraordinary piece. 10.00.

Antique Bronzes. Bronze lamp from the ruins of Pompeii. 20.00.

Pompeain Bronze. Fox. 15.00.

Pompeain Bronze. The Gladiator. 15.00.

Roman Bronze. Athlete. 10.00.

Japanese Bronze. Curious piece. 5.00.

Japanese Bronze. Angry Dragon. Very elaborate and magnificent specimen. 15.00.

Cloisonne Enamel Incense Burner. Parrot with removable wings. Enameled in colors on copper Choice piece. 10.00.

Antique Furniture. Very old Norwegian Cabinet. With beautifully carved panels, supported by richly carved columns, dated 1719. 85.00.

Very old Norwegian Church Chest. With two handsomely carved panels, representing the Adoration and the Presentation in the Temple, with arabesque design on side, surmounted on open base. Very remarkable piece, dated 1640. 125.00.

www.ingramcontent.com/pod-product-compliance
Lightning Source LLC
Chambersburg PA
CBHW022200020726
47496CB00008B/2803

* 9 7 8 3 7 4 2 8 3 2 0 8 5 *